WASHOE COUNTY LIBRARY
3 1235 03196 2322

D0016678

Fire in the Hills

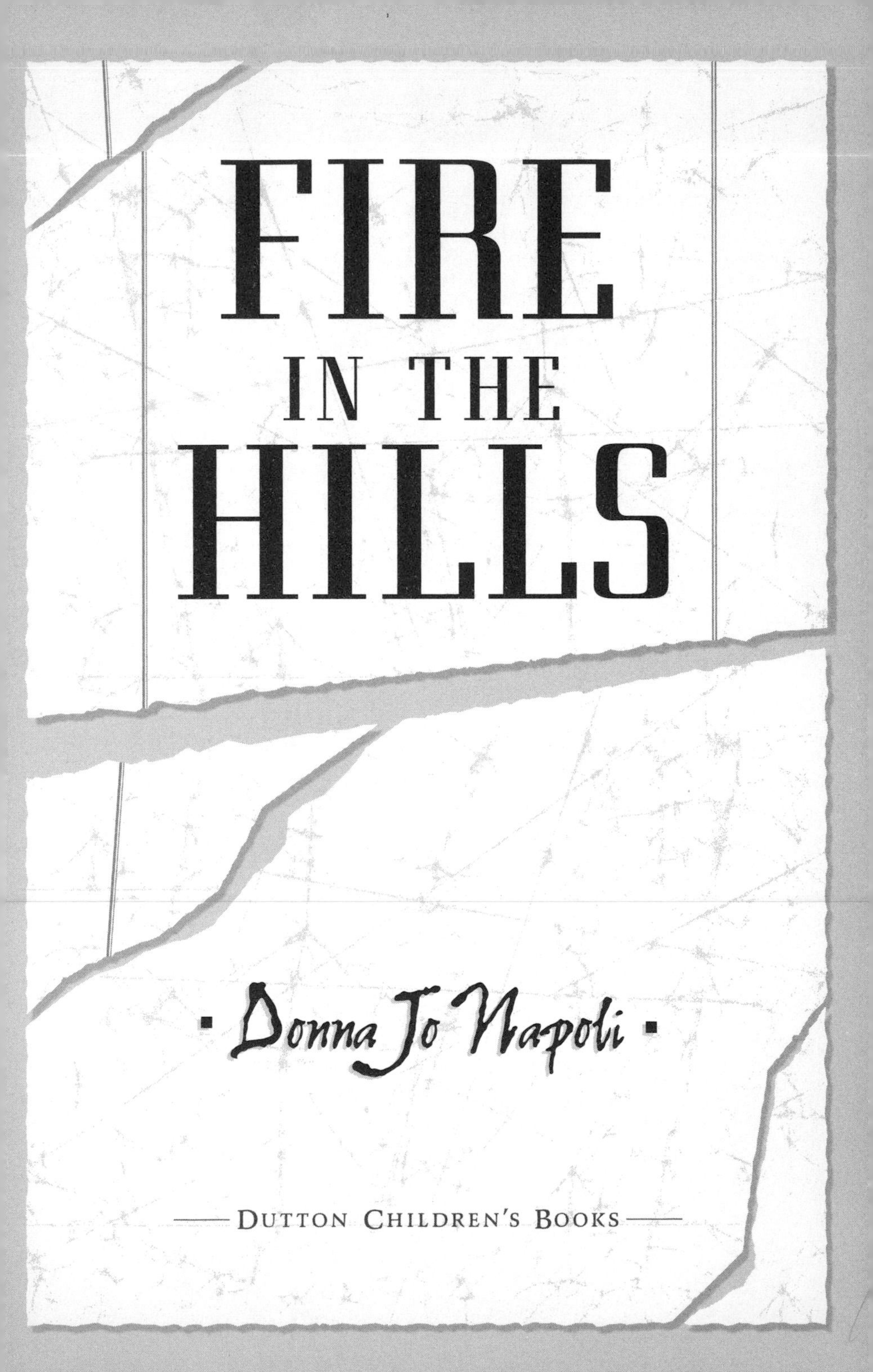

FIRE IN THE HILLS

· Donna Jo Napoli ·

DUTTON CHILDREN'S BOOKS

DUTTON CHILDREN'S BOOKS
A division of Penguin Young Readers Group

Published by the Penguin Group
Penguin Group (USA) Inc., 375 Hudson Street, New York, New York 10014, U.S.A. • Penguin Group (Canada), 90 Eglinton Avenue East, Suite 700, Toronto, Ontario, Canada M4P 2Y3 (a division of Pearson Penguin Canada Inc.) • Penguin Books Ltd, 80 Strand, London WC2R 0RL, England • Penguin Ireland, 25 St Stephen's Green, Dublin 2, Ireland (a division of Penguin Books Ltd) • Penguin Group (Australia), 250 Camberwell Road, Camberwell, Victoria 3124, Australia (a division of Pearson Australia Group Pty Ltd) • Penguin Books India Pvt Ltd, 11 Community Centre, Panchsheel Park, New Delhi - 110 017, India • Penguin Group (NZ), Cnr Airborne and Rosedale Roads, Albany, Auckland 1310, New Zealand (a division of Pearson New Zealand Ltd) • Penguin Books (South Africa) (Pty) Ltd, 24 Sturdee Avenue, Rosebank, Johannesburg 2196, South Africa • Penguin Books Ltd, Registered Offices: 80 Strand, London WC2R 0RL, England

Library of Congress Cataloging-in-Publication Data
Napoli, Donna Jo, date.
Fire in the hills / Donna Jo Napoli. — 1st ed.
p. cm.
Sequel to: Stones in water.
Summary: Upon returning to Italy, fourteen-year-old Roberto struggles to survive, first on his own, then as a member of the resistance, fighting against the Nazi occupiers while yearning to reach home safely and for an end to the war.
ISBN 0-525-47751-9
1. World War, 1939–1945—Italy—Juvenile fiction. [1. World War, 1939–1945—Italy—Fiction. 2. World War, 1939–1945—Underground movements—Italy—Fiction. 3. Survival—Fiction. 4. Italy—History—German occupation, 1943–1945—Fiction.] I. Title.
PZ7.N15Fir 2006
[Fic]–dc22 2005036721

Published in the United States by Dutton Children's Books,
a division of Penguin Young Readers Group
345 Hudson Street, New York, New York 10014
www.penguin.com/youngreaders

Designed by Jason Henry
Printed in USA * First Edition
1 3 5 7 9 10 8 6 4 2

To the spirit of Giuseppe Grandinetti, my Uncle Joe, who fought in World War II

ACKNOWLEDGMENTS

Thanks to the many librarians who helped me amass reading materials, and to Bill Reynolds, who did that as well as giving comments on this story. Thanks to Barry Furrow, for reading chapters as I wrote them—also to Robert and Eva, ever loyal. Thanks to Katie Ailes, Paolo Asso, Libby Chrissy, Leila Goldnick, Zach James, Hilary O'Connell, Beatrice Rubin, Richard Tchen, all of whom gave comments on earlier versions. Thanks to Annette Murphy-Shaw and her sixth-grade reading class at Holyoke Elementary School in Holyoke, Colorado, in spring 2005. Thanks to Eleanor Salgado's and Mary Reindorp's fourth-period eighth-grade language arts classes at the Strath Haven Middle School in Wallingford, Pennsylvania, in spring 2005. Thanks to Michael Sawyer and his eighth-grade language arts classes at the Ira Jones Middle School in Plainfield, Illinois, in spring 2005. Finally, thank you to my incomparable editor, Lucia Monfried.

Fire in the Hills

· 1 ·

ROBERTO STOOD ON THE DECK of the American warship and peered through the dark. A quarter moon glowed in the middle of so many bright stars.

Yes. There it was. Finally. The faintest outline, but unmistakable—the coast of Sicily. The island at the very bottom of Italy. He was coming home, at last.

His fingers curled around the smooth metal rail beside a cannon, and he smiled into the warm air. He'd come so far already. He could do this final short stretch—just Sicily to the mainland, then north to Venice. He was almost there—almost safe.

Maybe Mamma was in the kitchen right now, with the radio on, listening to war news like she always did. But she wouldn't hear anything that could make her guess where he was. Never in a million years. America was the enemy—there's no way anyone could have dreamed he'd wind up getting a ride back home on an American ship.

Soldiers passed, putting on helmets as they went. Someone handed one to Roberto. He tightened the strap under his neck and remembered the warning one of the American soldiers had given: "The waters are full of floating mines. If they hit us, swim against the tide—'cause the mines will be going wherever the tides go."

Mines floating in the sea.

But, with any luck, Roberto wouldn't have to worry about them. The Germans didn't know the Americans were coming. His ship would land, and he'd run away. Then hitch a ride. And another. And another. He'd be home in a couple of days, a week at most.

Still, Roberto tightened the helmet strap even more.

The storm that had wracked the night was well over, but a sudden sea breeze hit like a final gulp. It cooled Roberto's bare chest. He stood tall and breathed deep and felt stronger than ever.

It was midsummer, more than a year since he'd been kidnapped by the Germans for forced labor. A fuzz had formed over his upper lip. His birthday had come and gone; he was fourteen. He hadn't taken a moment to think about that till now. What must his parents have felt, seeing his birthday pass and having no idea where he was, if he was even alive? Well, on his next birthday, he'd have Mamma's famous cake. He could almost hear them singing, almost smell the burning wax of birthday candles, almost taste the creamy hazelnut filling.

A destroyer off to the right caught his attention; it foundered in the high surf. Someone opened fire. That's all it took, a single shot; instantly more shots came from everywhere.

His own ship let off volley after volley. Guns and cannons from all sides. He clung to the railing now. This couldn't last. When no one onshore shot back, the Americans would stop.

But they didn't stop.

The air itself seemed to explode. Each quick yellow flash was followed by a snow-white column of smoke that streamed up into the sky and blew away. The smoke got so thick, clouds sat on the water.

Droning came from overhead. Loud and fast. Roberto could see them against the faint moonlight—nineteen, twenty, more. Twin-engine planes droning droning. German bombers. What? This wasn't how it was supposed to be. No. Everything was going wrong. He was in the middle of a battle again—again again again. No!

It poured bombs.

The soldier beside Roberto fell to his knees, muttering. Praying?

Roberto clenched his teeth so hard, his eardrums hurt.

A bomb hit the destroyer in front of them. Flames shot

upward, then across the ship. When they reached the ammunition cargo, it exploded. Heat hit him like a thick curtain. Sweat broke out on his head and chest and back. It stung his eyes. The bright light of the blaze illuminated the ships. Roberto had had no idea there were so many of them, strung out in a line along the coast. This was a massive operation. And he realized with a gasp that all these boats were easy targets for the German planes now.

Another destroyer opened fire on the failing ship. Shooting at their own? But they had to—of course they had to. They needed the dark again. Only the ship was too close to shore, the water was already too shallow, the ship wouldn't sink. They were all sitting ducks.

A muffled explosion came from immediately behind them. Water mushroomed into the air, spraying the deck of Roberto's ship, soaking everyone. They'd just been bombed—the plane had missed, but only barely. And more planes were coming, more bombs.

On the beach mortar shells sent clouds of sand and smoke billowing up white, then turning black. When it cleared the littlest bit, Roberto saw people running for cover. Flames from buildings poked up red and yellow along the curve of beach. An ambulance screamed. Guns shot in staccato. Everything Roberto could make out onshore turned to rubble.

One of the Landing Ship Tanks in Roberto's convoy was already onshore. The tanks rolled off in file. Roberto's LST headed straight in, its guns blasting. Soldiers manned the tanks and trucks on the deck, getting ready to roll them out onto the land.

Suddenly his ship stopped, broached on a sandbar. The soldiers shouted to one another in confusion.

Roberto looked over the side. He wouldn't think about the mines in the water. His best chance was to act fast.

He took off the American military boots he'd been given. He threw off his helmet and life jacket. He didn't want anything that tied him to this war. He had to get away. To get home.

He jumped over the side. His hands and knees sank into the wet sand. A wave broke over him. He choked on salt water.

2

SWIM. Swim for an isolated spot of shore. But there were way too many ships along way too much of the coast. And the water was so greasy with diesel oil from sinking ships that swimming was unbearably hard.

Roberto focused his eyes straight for shore and refused to let anything else catch his attention. When his feet hit ground, he ran inland, past frantic masses of men struggling with jeeps stuck in the sand, heaving their weight and cursing. Bullets went every direction. People shouted. Mortar shells exploded in the sand beside him. He ran.

Over the noise of everything else, ship bells clanged. Roberto looked back for an instant. A plane burned on the surface of the water. The ship beside it was half-underwater.

He ran faster, almost blindly, beyond the little cluster of buildings that seemed to be all this town was made of. He kept running through dry grasses, across a barren plain.

Distance—all he wanted to do was put distance between himself and the crack of rifles, the boom of bombs and cannons. Then he stumbled over something warm and hard—the metal of a rail, a train rail—and he felt like he'd been smacked in the head with reason.

Walking on the ties made good sense. It would be easier on his bare feet. They were already covered with cuts from ragged stones. He wouldn't be able to walk at all if he didn't give them a little protection—the protection the ties could afford. And the rails would eventually lead to Messina, the port town that was closest to the mainland of Italy. From there he'd find a way to cross the strait and head home. This was the answer. Yes.

He followed the tracks at a run, till he missed a tie and fell again, slamming his jaw on the dense wood. He got up and forced himself to move carefully. Formations of planes still passed above. But no one was following him, he was sure of that by now. It was okay to go slow. He picked his way with as much precision as the dark allowed.

The spacing of the ties was regular, and soon the swing of his arms helped him move without thought. His steps were like a pulse—thud, thud, thud—in the beast that was this night.

Morning eventually spread light from his left. That meant he was going south—he'd thought so, but he'd gotten so disoriented in his mad dash, that he hadn't been entirely sure. No planes had passed overhead for a while. The battle noises still came from a distance, behind and to the right, but muffled. He stopped a moment and looked back. Black smoke rose against the dawn sky.

A huge lizard clung to the rail maybe seven or eight meters in front of him, its tail stretched out full length. Roberto's approach must have woken it, for it turned its head and stared, as though daring him.

Roberto didn't know anything about lizards really, but he didn't think they would hurt you. Still, this was the lizard's territory, not his. He left the train tracks and made a wide semicircle around the lizard, then went back to walking on the ties. The lizard never budged.

Not much later, Roberto made out buildings ahead. He stopped and watched: white homes of neatly stacked stone blocks with worn stone staircases that wound up the outside of them—all so different from Venice. A town spread out beyond them. No people were on the streets, just a pair of stray dogs.

Well, of course not. Anyone with sense would be hiding. The explosions weren't that far away.

Did he dare go with the tracks right into the center of town? He needed water. And something to eat. And maybe a place to rest out of the sun.

He left the train ties and skirted around the edge of town, watching, listening. He didn't see a single uniform. He didn't hear a word of German.

Why should he be afraid then? This was Italy, after all. His homeland, at last. The people behind these doors were Italian civilians. His countrymen. And he was a kid, alone, clearly unarmed; there was nowhere on him to hide a weapon.

He turned down a street and ran his fingertips along walls covered with posters of Prime Minister Mussolini's head in a helmet, gazing far off, as if at the future. Stamped under each head was the word *Duce*—duke. Everyone called Mussolini the Duke, the leader of the military. Beside each head were fighting words, urging the people on, ending with, "*Se muoio, vendicatemi*—if I die, take revenge for me." Brutal words.

Roberto pulled away in revulsion. He knew what Mussolini was all about. No one should fight for Mussolini.

Crash.

A man came tumbling out a door, slamming onto the sidewalk not a body length in front of Roberto. He wore a uniform.

Roberto turned and ran.

He didn't stop till he was far outside town. He could still see the train tracks from here. That was enough. He'd follow them from this distance.

The ground was mostly dry grass, raspy weeds, small rocks. He walked.

He walked all the rest of the morning.

Farmhouses were scattered across the plain. Beside one was an artichoke field. The artichokes had been cut already, but the farmer had left a few to blossom. Large purple flowers stuck up here and there. Mamma would have loved the sight.

Most of the farmhouses had small kitchen gardens right outside the door. Roberto got close enough to one to make out beans and zucchini. His chest swelled with need, his skin prickled. But the thought of who might live there numbed him again.

He walked all afternoon.

The mistral wind blew steadily, so he never got terribly hot. That was a lucky thing. Everyone knew Sicily could scorch you in the summer. Yes, that was lucky. He was lucky. He was alone and hungry and thirsty and empty-handed. But he was alive, in his own country, on a path that would take him home. And the wind blew.

He heard the rumble of the train before he saw it. He ran for the cover of a bush and flattened himself on the ground. Trains carried the military, and he wouldn't get near a soldier again. Ever.

When it was out of sight, he stood. But he'd moved too fast, and his mouth was too dry; his head spun. He fell.

It was hard to get up. He lifted his chest, but it was hard. He was tired. So tired. And, after all, this place was as good as any—because no place was safe. Not really.

He let his cheek fall back onto the hot dirt.

He slept.

· 3 ·

When Roberto woke, the sun told him it was already midmorning. He'd slept . . . what? Maybe fifteen hours. Maybe more. He sat up slowly, careful not to rush anything. It was time to think clearly. Figure things out.

The corners of his mouth cracked. His tongue felt large and raspy.

Water. The first priority was water.

Where were the rivers around here? Sicily had rivers, he knew that from his old school lessons. Did they dry up in summer?

Those people in the farmhouses the day before had to get their water from somewhere.

Wells.

He got to his feet and brushed off. A slight nausea made him pause to breathe deep. It passed, but he was still light-headed. And the air felt funny in his ears—buzzy like insects. He walked, looking, looking.

It wasn't long before he saw another farmhouse. Isolated. With a well to one side.

A well in a dry land was maybe the most valuable commodity a person had. Who knew what trouble he could get in for taking water without asking first?

A tree behind the well hung heavy with yellow-orange fruits. Apricots? Were they ripe?

He watched a while. No one came out. No one went in.

He couldn't just stand there forever. In fact, he felt like he couldn't stand there for a moment more. His knees wobbled. He was nauseated. Such a short while without water could do this?

Well, sure. People died without water. Especially in the sun. Besides, he hadn't eaten, either.

He went up to the door and knocked.

"What do you want?" came a woman's shout.

"Water," called back Roberto, trying to make his voice sound trustworthy. A woman. A woman was less likely to have a gun. He screwed up his courage. "And food. Bread. An apricot or two. I could work for it."

"You're not Sicilian, what are you doing here?"

"I . . . I was in a battle."

"What battle? Where?"

"On the coast."

"Which town?"

"I don't know."

"What do you mean, you don't know? How can you not know?"

Her questions were like fists; his answers, like limp hands. Against all odds, though, the exchange invigorated Roberto. He was speaking his own language again, finally. And it didn't matter that the woman behind the door spoke Sicilian dialect, not Venetian, and not standard Italian. His ears were so greedy for a familiar language that he didn't have trouble following it.

"I haven't had a drop to drink for almost two days. Please. I'll work for you. I promise."

The woman opened the door a crack: drawn face, hair pulled back tightly, black eyes that gave nothing away.

Roberto raised his hands in surrender, as Maurizio had taught him to do way back in Turkey. Maurizio, who was dead now, who Roberto had refused to let himself think about. His hands took on such a sudden heaviness, he feared he'd fall forward.

"Put your hands down," the woman said breathily, as though she was the weary one. "What can you do for me?"

"What do you need done?"

She stood back and let him pass inside and poured him a

glass of water. A second. A third. Then she led him to a field and pointed.

Two boys cut wheat. They were kids, around eight and ten, no older, for sure. The woman turned without a word and went back to the farmhouse.

Roberto walked up behind the boys. They'd given him a quick glance when he was standing with the woman, but now they worked as though he wasn't there. Sweat dripped down their backs. Their hair gleamed with it. They'd already cut about half the field. They must have been working since dawn. Or maybe they'd cut the day before, too.

There were only two scythes. What was Roberto supposed to use? He stood empty-handed, feeling like an idiot.

"Make bundles," said the older boy, between swings of the scythe.

Roberto bent and gathered cut wheat in his arms.

"No, stupid. Roll it. Show him, Piero."

The littler boy dropped his scythe and rolled the cut wheat along the ground, gathering more as he went.

Roberto rolled wheat into bundles and left them at the end of each row of wheat. He rolled and rolled until his neck and back ached from bending over.

"Here." Piero handed him his scythe and took over rolling.

So Roberto cut wheat. It was harder than it looked, and Piero was clearly stronger than he looked.

After a few hours, the woman called from the edge of the field. The boys dropped what they were doing and ran. Roberto followed.

The table was already set. The boys washed their hands and faces and sat on the benches, with forks ready. The midday meal was whole young artichokes, boiled and flavored with vinegar. And a bowl of spaghetti with fresh tomatoes. And apricots.

The boys talked a little, but Roberto hardly heard them. He ate till his stomach hurt.

"Rest now," said the woman. "You've earned it."

The boys obediently trooped into another room to nap.

"No one can work in the heat of the afternoon," said the woman. She carried the dirty plates to the sink.

Roberto wasn't sure what to do next. He stood uncertainly.

"Sit back down. You stay there."

He sat and watched her.

She returned to the table and stood over the bowl of water the last few apricots were floating in. She picked one up and dried it with her dishcloth. She rolled it round and round, round and round. It was long past dry. Little bits of the skin were coming off now. If she kept doing that, the whole thing would come apart. She stopped at last and said, "Did you see Carlino?"

Roberto blinked in confusion.

"My son." She put the apricot on the table, wiped her hands

on the dishcloth now, and sat beside Roberto. "He's taller than you. A bit stouter. His hair curls like yours. He's in uniform, of course, like all the others. But he has a wonderful smile. If you saw his smile, you'd pick him out." Her words raced with sudden urgency. "You'd recognize him. Like an angel."

Roberto rubbed his lips and pretended to search his memory, but, really, he wondered if she was crazy. How could he explain to her that he hadn't looked at anyone's face? How could he explain the chaos of battle?

But he wouldn't explain it to her even if he could. It wouldn't help anyone to know something that horrible.

He couldn't look her in the eyes at first.

When he finally dared to, though, he found her eyes weren't on him anymore. They stared past him. She got up without waiting for an answer and opened the door.

It took a few moments for Roberto to realize she wanted him to leave. A lump formed in his throat. But it shouldn't have. He hadn't wanted to stay. Not really. It was the lure of food that made his fingers curl under this bench and hold on tight. And the lure of a home. And a woman's voice.

But the sooner he left, the sooner he'd be on the path toward his real home, his real mother.

As he went out the door, the woman said, "Don't put your hands up in surrender when someone opens their door. Act like a half-wit, instead. It's hard to have mercy, but easy to have pity."

·4·

ROBERTO STOOD ON A HILLTOP and looked down at the battleships moored in the wide harbor of the city below. Soldiers in tan milled around the waterfront. Those were British uniforms, he was sure of it. He'd seen them in war newsreels back in Venice, so long ago. Sun glinted off their helmets.

He'd heard the battle two nights before. He'd slept outdoors in the scratchy dry scrub of these foothills and squeezed his eyes shut against the glare of the explosions and rocked from side to side on the ground till the noises finally ceased and sleep finally came. The next day he'd sat there, unable to get himself to move. But he had to move today. The need for water was that simple. He had to.

He wasn't sure how long it had been since he first set foot in Sicily. He'd lost track of the days. But one thing he knew, this was taking longer than he'd hoped.

His plan had been to march as many hours as he could,

always within sight of the train tracks, and stop only when he absolutely needed water, food, or sleep. But explosions interrupted the plan. They came at any hour of the night or day, always from the direction of the coast. A day might pass without them, but then they'd return. And every time he trembled and ran for the hills. If he was lucky enough to find a cave, he stayed there. Longer than he should have. Once, he found a cave with a stream inside it, and he stayed for three whole days.

He couldn't understand his own behavior. The night the American warship had brought him to Sicily, he'd run straight through the middle of guns and bombs on that beach. Past flames and wounded, screaming men. Past mutilated bodies. Now the guns and bombs were distant, yet now he trembled worse each time he heard them. He couldn't help it; he couldn't win against his mounting terror. It immobilized him. Not even the pounding drive to get home could get him going again. Only the need for food—the fundamental need for survival—finally spurred him on.

The battles weren't the only reason his plan for getting home wasn't working out, though. Even without that hateful noise in the distance, he couldn't walk for more than a few hours at a time. His strength was failing; hunger sapped his energy.

It wasn't for shortage of farmhouses. No, he'd gotten used to rubbing his lips and pretending to think—the half-wit, struggling to seize on a vague memory—while women talked at him, always women. Everyone worried about a son, a brother, a father, a nephew, each one sent out by the Fascists to fight the Allied powers, because . . . because . . . Because that's what you did. You fought, even if you couldn't remember why.

He worked hard for these women—repairing roofs, lugging stones for walls, picking cactus pears, anything they wanted. But they were increasingly poor. They gave him a tomato. Or a lemon to suck on. Or dried figs, crunchy with wasp bodies. Or olives. He gnawed on rock-hard brown bread and tried to fool his empty stomach into not twisting, while he listened respectfully as the women talked and scratched behind the long ears of Nubian goats, their eyes limpid with held-back tears.

They talked of the Allies gobbling up Sicily. They welcomed each invasion, because the more battles won, the sooner this cursed war would end and their men could come home.

Welcome invasions. Incomprehensible.

Roberto spied a sign over on the road. He walked across the hillside and read it. It was hard to believe: that city down there was Siracusa. Great Siracusa had fallen to the Allies.

Roberto hugged himself and watched the scene in the city below. Smoke still rose from a cathedral on fire. People rushed in and out of a large army hospital tent set up in a piazza.

Other people cheered in the streets. They threw flowers from windows down under the feet of the British soldiers.

Welcome invasions.

It was already noon or later. And Roberto hadn't eaten anything but wild fennel and carrots for days. He needed to knock on a door soon.

He walked along the road till he came to a house set back a ways. He knocked.

The woman opened the door without asking who it was. The very act chilled him.

She looked him up and down and smiled. It seemed she almost expected him. "Come in."

On the table was a bowl of broth with bread soaking in it and a spoon tipping out. He'd interrupted her meal, sparse as it was. His mouth watered. He forced his eyes away.

The woman clapped her hands together once, a sound that made Roberto wince, and moved briskly about the kitchen. She set water to boiling and took a jar of something from her pantry and heated it and put out a second bowl, but this one with a fork beside it. She talked as she worked. She muttered about prices.

Roberto strained to hear. He wanted to appear polite. He wanted not to stare at the stuff she'd put in the pot, not to think only about the fact that she'd put out a fork—a fork for something solid, not just a spoon.

"The cost of pasta has tripled since the war began. Did

you realize that? You're a country boy and you don't know how prices work, of course, but you know that's bad, don't you?" She didn't pause long enough for Roberto to answer. "The cost of oil has multiplied by eight. Bread, by five. It's killing us. Day by day." She looked at him and nodded.

He nodded back instinctively. And he felt like a liar. If he opened his mouth and his accent revealed he wasn't from Sicily, would she throw him out?

But she didn't ask him anything. Not what he was doing there, who he was. Not what he could offer in exchange. Nothing.

Roberto stood, mesmerized by the smells that came from the stove, by the movements of the woman's arm as she stirred, by her words that went counter to her cooking. He had to press his lips together to keep his jaw from hanging open.

"Sit now."

He sat at the table, and she placed a heavenly bowl of pasta with sardines in front of him.

He ate.

She took out a bottle of oil and poured a dollop in Roberto's bowl. "My son worked in town for a month to buy that oil on the black market."

So why was she giving him this precious food? Roberto felt guilty about eating it. But he was too hungry to stop. And he knew in his bones that the woman couldn't bear it if he stopped.

She sat across from him now, and her hand ran up and down that oil bottle, up and down, up and down. Her voice was thin as a blade of dry mountain grass. She'd crush to powder with the least bit of pressure. She needed protection—somebody strong.

A heart-piercing sense of déjà vu made Roberto pause, his fork halfway to his mouth. The first woman who had fed him rolled an apricot in her dishcloth. This one ran her hand up and down the oil bottle. They were variations on a theme, music that snaked inside his head.

Only this woman didn't ask if he'd seen anyone. Oh, Lord.

When he finished eating, she told him to nap on the kitchen floor while she went inside. He waited till he didn't hear any movement beyond the door, long enough that she was probably asleep—he hoped she was asleep, at least—then sneaked out and returned to following the train tracks at a distance.

Home, he keened to himself to drown out the desolate, crying music of the women, all these women, home home home home. Every step took him closer.

5

ROBERTO WANDERED THE STREETS of Messina, looking for an opportunity. He'd walked all the way here on feet that now were so callused they were numb as stumps. And there it was: a storage shed with an unlocked door. He squeezed past ropes and canvas into a corner, squatted, and slept instantly.

The next morning he woke early. He stretched as best he could, without knocking anything over, and slipped out into the empty predawn streets before the owner of the shed could come and scold him. He turned up the narrowest alley he could find and leaned against a wall. It wasn't as narrow as the alleys in Venice—he couldn't touch both sides at once—but it felt good to stand there anyway.

The city was quiet. Whoever stirred inside these homes moved like cats. No one wanted to be noticed. Of course not. That was the trick these days—blend into the background, disappear.

And that was another reason why he liked narrow alleys. The dawn sun didn't reach him here. If someone glanced up this alley, they wouldn't see him unless he moved.

Roberto looked down the length of the alley, out to the cement walkway along the water, where two Nazi officers leaned over a metal railing and peered through binoculars. One of them had a grenade tucked into the top of his boot.

The day before, when Roberto had first walked the train tracks into Messina, he'd watched steamers carry retreating Italian soldiers across that water to the mainland of Italy. Now it looked like German soldiers were going to retreat, too, otherwise what were those officers doing there?

The land on the other side of the strait was easily visible, the hulk of a hill blue against the rising gray of morning. It was far, but not that far. And every single boat crossing the strait was full of soldiers, every single one of which he wanted to avoid. That's why Roberto had finally decided he had to swim it. Maybe tonight.

He was a good swimmer. Most Venetian boys were. He'd never swum that far before, but he could float when he needed a rest. It wasn't that far.

He'd been in Sicily probably two months by now—at least two months. He had to get off this island, on the road home. Yes, he'd swim the strait tonight.

"Want to make some money?"

Roberto had learned not to flinch at unexpected voices. It

made you look suspect, and worse—smart. He turned slowly and assumed that vacant look in the eye that had served him well in Sicily so far.

The voice belonged to an Italian soldier with a festering cut across his face, high on his right temple, through the red ball oozing pus that was his eye, to the flange of his nostril. "Take me home with you," he said. "Just till the Allies get here and I can surrender. It won't be long." His accent made Roberto think of Maurizio; he was Roman, for sure. Another Roman deserter.

Roberto shook his head.

The soldier grabbed him around the throat with both hands. "Take me home, or I'll kill you."

"I don't have a home here," croaked Roberto. He yanked down on the man's elbows and broke his grip. It wasn't hard; the soldier was as weak as he looked.

The soldier absently ran the fingers of his left hand over his grimy front teeth. "You're not even Sicilian. Listen to you. You're Venetian, right? What are you doing here? A kid like you. Hell, you didn't make the mistake of actually joining the army, did you? Idiot. Complete idiot." And he cried. His shoulders curled forward, and his head slumped and he bawled.

Roberto quickly stepped close. "Don't do that," he whispered. "People will look at us. We'll get caught."

The man put his hands over his mouth and nose. His body jerked with sobs. But he didn't make noise anymore.

"Listen," said Roberto softly, "I wish I could help you, but I can't. I'm going home, to Venice, and I'm going to swim that strait. You aren't strong enough to make it."

"Swim the strait?" The man dropped his arms as though they were dead things. The stench of his breath made Roberto turn his head away. "And then what? Walk into the hands of the Germans?"

What did he mean? "Once I get on the other side, I'll never have to look at another German again."

"Don't you know anything? Haven't you heard?" The man clutched Roberto's arm. "Back in July the Allies made an air raid on Rome. A thousand civilians died. One thousand. The people couldn't stand it anymore. They're fed up with the war. They threw stones at the king, so he had Mussolini arrested."

"Arrested?" Roberto couldn't have heard right. "Prime Minister Mussolini's in prison?" The famous duke in prison?

"You bet. People danced in the streets when Mussolini fell. Let that devil rot."

"So we're with the Allies now?" asked Roberto.

"If only! The king stayed with the Nazis. But Hitler hates us now—he always did, only now it's in the open. And the Allies hate us, too. The whole thing's a mess. The army has gone to hell. No one has ammunition or food." The soldier shook Roberto's arm passionately. "In these past few weeks the Germans have occupied us to keep Italy from being used for Allied bases. They've occupied us. Like they occupied France. They're all over Italy, all the way down to Naples."

Roberto's stomach clenched. "Are the Germans in Venice?" Were his parents okay?

"Ihr da! Halt! Was macht ihr eigentlich?"

Roberto instantly pressed his back to the wall and turned his head to face the German soldier, who pointed a pistol at them. It was the officer with the grenade in his boot. He didn't have to say it again—Roberto wasn't about to move.

"Wir sprechen eben," Roberto said, hoping that meant "We're just talking"—his German was so poor, despite all the time he'd spent with Germans over the past year. He tried to keep a calm tone.

But the German officer's eyes were hard on the Italian soldier. Roberto dared to look at the Italian beside him. He had raised his hands in surrender. How dumb of him! By raising his hands, he was admitting he was a deserter. Roberto knew too well what Nazis did to Italian deserters—what they'd done to Maurizio.

Roberto moved closer to the Italian soldier. *"Verwunden und verlegen*—He's dazed and confused," he said. He held out his hands toward the German officer in plea. But hands couldn't help enough; German words were too hard to get out of his mouth. He gave up and spoke in Italian: "With his eye all messed up, he can hardly see you. He doesn't know what he's doing."

The officer shot the Italian soldier in the head.

Roberto jumped backward in reflex. His head smacked against the wall. His mouth stuck open in silent horror.

"Komm mit!"

Roberto stared stupidly at the crumpled heap of soldier. Blood pooled under his head. Roberto couldn't do anything for him now. No one could.

"Komm mit!" It was a shout now.

But Roberto didn't want to leave the Italian soldier. He couldn't just leave him there. Like garbage.

The German officer grabbed Roberto by the arm and pulled him, stumbling, down the alley.

They came out on the waterfront. German troops flowed onto the docks from every street and alley. They streamed into ferries that had suddenly appeared. And other kinds of boats, too—steamboats, and motor rafts.

Hundreds of German soldiers crossed the strait. Thousands. Crowded and crushed and crazy.

Roberto crossed with them, his hands tied behind his back, his vision blood red.

· 6 ·

THE TRAIN PULLED INTO NAPLES in the middle of the morning. "Get ready," Kurt, the German officer, said to Roberto in that clipped German of his. He took the cigar out from between his teeth and dropped it on the train floor. "The people in this city are stupid. They don't know a word of German. You say something as simple as '*Halt*,' and they keep on walking. So you're my voice on everything here."

Sure. Roberto could do that. In the four days since he'd been with these Nazis they'd taken him all the way to Naples, and the only thing he'd had to do in return was translate Kurt's orders into Italian. That wasn't being part of the war—not a big part, anyway—not an unforgivable part. He could bear this. After Kurt had shot the Roman deserter back in Messina, Roberto had seen no more murders. The worst part, really, was having to listen to German again. Night and day—Kurt's continual barking.

So, really, this was okay—Roberto could do this. As long as they kept heading north with him, north toward Venice, and as long as the orders he had to translate were just telling people to get out of the way, he'd do what Kurt wanted—he'd be his translator. He was going home, and riding on a train or in a German truck was faster than walking. They hadn't stayed anyplace more than a night so far. Hopefully, they'd be out of Naples within a day or two.

Roberto jumped off the train with the German troops, and all of them filed up an empty road. They turned a corner, and he tripped over a block of stone and fell. He couldn't catch himself because his hands were still tied at his back. Debris covered the road. It seemed every other building was crumbling. This part of town had been bombed out completely. No wonder the roads were empty. This one was barely passable.

Another officer led them off the road and through winding alleys—each one as silent and empty as the last one—to the next fairly large street, where a small procession passed. Italian men walked in pairs, one behind the other. Their thin, bare chests glistened with sweat, though the day was hardly hot. Between them they carried armchairs mounted on two long poles. A wounded German soldier sat in each chair. The German troops from the train stopped and saluted as the procession went by.

Kurt walked alongside one of the chairs, pulling Roberto

with him. "What's happening?" he asked the German soldier in the chair.

"We're going to Pompei to play tourists for the day."

"You deserve the royal treatment," said Kurt. He slipped a cigar into the shirt pocket of the soldier.

The soldier took his arm out of the big sling. "Royalty without a hand." He waved his stump. "One hundred and twenty air raids those damned Allies made on this city. One hundred and twenty."

Kurt shook his head in disgust.

Roberto looked around at the ruins with new eyes. It wasn't just this part of town that had been bombed. One hundred and twenty air raids—the whole city must be in shambles. How many bombs did the Allies have, anyway?

How many people had the Allies killed?

They went up the road and passed a wall with the same poster over and over: Mussolini standing tall, heels together in high black boots, his right arm raised in salute above his helmet. The prime minister might be off in prison somewhere, but the Nazis who occupied this city had kept his pictures up.

They came to a piazza filled with German tanks, striped like tigers, immobile, colossal iron monsters. The troops crossed the piazza and, without a glance, filed past boys who were wearing nothing but shorts—like Roberto—playing harmonicas. Empty cans sat on the ground in front of the boys—for coins. They were scrawny little things with gleaming eyes, like clever stray cats. Roberto looked at them, and they stared back.

The troops marched into a big hotel.

"Headquarters," said Kurt to Roberto as they followed. "Comfortable ones."

"Welcome!" An officer came running to Kurt, a huge smile of recognition on his face. They hugged.

"So how is it here?" asked Kurt.

"Not so bad."

"The Sicilians were sneaky," said Kurt. "The men hid to avoid fighting. Sometimes they even turned on us and gave the Allies information. So I know how it can be. Tell me about the Neapolitans. Tell me the truth."

"The truth?" The officer's mouth went up in a smirk. "These people have no spunk. No fight at all. Someone does something against orders, you shoot him. Someone looks at you funny, you shoot him. Someone stands there and you just don't like the size of his nose, you shoot him. And the rest do nothing but scurry back into their rat holes. These people—they've got no spine." He leaned close. "And they're desperate. At mealtime stick a loaf of bread in your jacket, and you can use it tonight if you don't want to sleep alone. The women sell themselves for less than that. You can have two at once if you want." He smacked his lips. "Wait till you see what a fourteen-year-old Neapolitan girl looks like. Starvation can be a beautiful thing." He laughed.

Kurt laughed, too. "Which way to the commander?"

The officer pointed. "See you at lunch?" He winked.

Kurt had to push Roberto along, he was too stunned to move on his own. A fourteen-year-old Neapolitan girl. Selling herself for a piece of bread. A girl his age. The center of his chest burned. He doubled over coughing.

"Colonel Scholl." Kurt saluted.

"Good to see you. We'll talk later. Right now I've got to find someone with a translator to get over to the jail." Scholl was already striding past.

"I have a translator. This boy here."

Scholl spun on his heel. "Really?" He looked at Roberto, then back at Kurt. "Here's the situation. A rogue group of university students—all riffraff—staged a protest against the German occupation last week. We had them arrested, and today the whole lot is to be interrogated."

Kurt stood at attention. "Where's the jail, sir?"

Scholl gave a close-lipped smile. "Out the door, turn right, and keep going. I don't know how many streets. Maybe ten. Twelve. It's one of the few undamaged buildings. You won't miss it."

So Roberto found himself back out on the empty streets

again, in tow behind Kurt, who walked quickly, puffing on a new cigar.

They were several blocks from headquarters when a whoop came from a window. It tore through the silent air like lightning. A second whoop came from another window. And now cheers came from everywhere. A woman leaned out a small balcony and threw garbage on Kurt's head. Kurt shouted obscenities up at her, but his voice was drowned out. People poured from doorways, and the streets filled in a matter of minutes. Everyone shouted with joy.

Kurt threw his cigar in the street, grabbed Roberto by the arm, and raced back toward the hotel headquarters. "What are they saying? What's happening?"

"Italy surrendered," said Roberto, half-dazed. Could it be true? Everyone was shouting that Italy had surrendered to the Allies. The war was over. The Americans were coming, and the Germans would have to leave and life could go on. No more bombs. September 8 was a great great day. Could it really be true?

Kurt dragged Roberto along faster, his eyes darting every which way. They came to the wall they'd passed earlier. A group of half-naked boys, like the ones in the piazza earlier, ripped down the posters of Mussolini. A radio blared the news of the armistice from an open window above them. A boy stopped his ripping to spit at Kurt.

Kurt pulled out his gun automatically, then quick stuck it in Roberto's back and ran in panic, pushing Roberto ahead of him.

Nazi headquarters was in an uproar. Colonel Scholl gave orders and people rushed to burn documents and pack up. They worked all the rest of the day and into the night.

Roberto watched them from the corner where he tried to shrink away. His mind raced. Outside the cheering that had gone up with the announcement of the armistice had died. Roberto sidled over toward a window, working to hear. There was noise inside the room, so it was hard to be sure, but he thought the street outside was quiet. Were the people gathering to attack? Would they set the hotel on fire?

If only his hands were free, he could open a shutter. But, oh, he could reach the latch with his mouth. He leaned and closed his mouth over the metal ball on the latch.

Slap!

Roberto went flying sideways and the latch ripped the corner of his mouth. The side of his head cracked on the sharp edge of the window frame. He felt wet drip from his ear to his shoulder.

"Imbecile!" hissed the German soldier. "If you open the shutters, they'll be able to aim. We're targets, you revolting imbecile."

Roberto stumbled back to the corner. His ear throbbed.

His mouth burned at the side where it bled. He looked from face to face. They were all terrified.

They'd die in this hotel.

Roberto would die in this hotel.

He sank to the floor and shut his eyes.

· 7 ·

MORNING CAME. The hotel wasn't on fire. Not a shot had disturbed the silence outdoors.

Roberto rubbed his wrists. Kurt had untied him long enough to let him use a toilet, then eat a roll and a small chunk of cheese. It was hard to chew without breaking the scab at the corner of his mouth.

He picked the dried blood off his shoulder and neck. But he left his ear and the side of his mouth encrusted for fear he'd set them bleeding again.

Kurt came over. "Done eating then?" He retied Roberto's hands behind him.

Roberto retreated to his corner.

And that's how it went.

All day long.

They stayed inside the hotel, waiting. Someone speculated on what to do. Scholl squelched the discussion immediately. He said he wanted a quick getaway, of course, of course, but they had to wait for orders from Hitler. That was it. No more of that kind of talk.

The second day a man insisted he had to go out. And he needed a couple of volunteers to go with him. His truck was full of rifles, and if they didn't go unload them, the Italians would get them.

Scholl made the men who went outside put on white armbands as a precaution.

And everyone mumbled anxiously, worrying whether they'd make it back alive.

They did. And they were unharmed. Nothing even remotely threatening had happened to them.

So the next day Scholl sent out men wearing white armbands to get fresh water and food.

They made it back, too. With news this time. A German truck driver said he'd caught a band of orphans—the result of all those air raids—stealing food from his truck. But that was all. Hardly anything. No shots were fired.

When Roberto woke on the fourth morning, the atmosphere in the hotel headquarters had clearly changed. People spoke with bravura again. Several men ventured out.

At noon most came back. But one German soldier reported that a group of young men had taken his companions as prisoners, and he'd escaped only by pure luck.

That set Scholl to pacing. Then another soldier burst into headquarters with the news that the Italian general in charge of Naples had disbanded his soldiers. The general had told them all to go home, the war was over. And he had disappeared somewhere himself.

"Idiot!" Scholl smiled. "That excuse for a general probably is hiding in a convent somewhere. Up in the hills, I bet. Idiot coward!"

Everyone laughed.

And then Hitler's orders came over the telegraph wire. His fury at the Italians for signing the armistice with the Allies was like a volcano. He ordered Colonel Scholl to get his troops out of Naples, but first he was to reduce the city to mud and ashes. The Italians would learn what their treachery cost: mud and ashes.

Roberto sat in the corner and watched everything change in seconds. German soldiers threw away their white armbands and picked up submachine guns. They marched out into the streets, and Roberto was marched out with them, pulled along by Kurt.

Tanks rolled, loudspeakers declared a state of siege, first in German, then, through Roberto's mouth, in Italian. Colonel Scholl announced that no attacks on German soldiers would be tolerated. For each dead German, the people of Naples would pay one hundred times over.

The Neapolitans were given twenty-four hours to turn over their weapons. Kurt led Nazi soldiers from house to house looking for weapons, with Roberto translating all the way. But hardly anyone turned over anything except a few old historic swords, lying around as family heirlooms. In their anger, the Germans took watches and jewelry and, worst of all, what little food there was. They burned homes and businesses helter-skelter. Like Kurt said, that way no one felt safe, no matter what they did.

Then the Germans called the people out into a huge piazza. With one hand, a Nazi soldier dragged a young Italian man to the front of the crowd. No, he wasn't even a man, he was a boy, maybe a couple of years older than Roberto, a boy in sailor's clothes. In the Nazi's other hand was a suitcase. The boy screamed he was innocent. He screamed and screamed.

Boom! A cannon volley sounded, and a large building on the piazza caught fire. At the noise Roberto pressed his arms tight against his body to control the shakes. He heard someone at his side mutter in Italian, "Our university. Our wonderful university."

A Nazi officer ordered everyone to kneel. No one knew what he'd said, so Roberto had to pass the word—"Get on your knees, get on your knees, please."

A man in the crowd asked, "Do they make you kneel when they're going to shoot you?"

Roberto's breath caught. He didn't know. But there were many more Neapolitans there than Germans. If the Germans opened fire and if the people fought back, the Germans would lose. The Germans could do terrible things, but they wouldn't be that stupid. Would they?

The Nazi officer was screaming now, jumping in place, saying they all better get on their knees fast.

Then another Nazi shouted in mangled Italian. And everyone got to their knees. He said that boy had thrown grenades at German soldiers. He said the suitcase was full of grenades. He said the boy's punishment was that he had to go into the burning building—he'd get burned up.

The boy cried that he was innocent. He swore it on the name of the Holy Virgin. On the name of his mother. When the Nazi let go of his arm, he threw himself on the ground and howled.

"Do you need others to go with you? Is that what you want?" asked the Nazi.

The boy stood up. Mucus dangled from his chin. He shook all over. But he went. He went straight for the flaming doorway.

Roberto watched, horrified. He took a step after the boy, moving instinctively. But he stopped. The intense heat of the fire was like a wall, even here where he stood. The boy must already be in pain. And it would get hideous fast. "Please, Kurt," said Roberto. "Please."

Kurt looked at him a moment. Then he licked his bottom lip. "For you," he said. He shot the boy in the back. "You owe me now."

8

ROBERTO WALKED IN FRONT OF KURT, the tip of the German's pistol pressed against his back. Kurt barked orders in German to his soldiers and simply pushed aside Italians who got in the way. But he wanted Roberto there as translator just in case; now and then an Italian might be useful, after all.

The Nazis ransacked the great museum.

They burned factories.

They burned homes.

That was the first week. Roberto's head hurt all the time. He couldn't sleep. He barely ate. But he stumbled on. This would end. The Americans were coming. The Germans had to get out of Naples soon. This would end.

The second week they blew up one of the few aqueducts that was still standing. Water—no more water.

The wells of Naples couldn't supply enough for everyone, anyone could see that. When Roberto was in Sicily, he'd gone only a couple of days at a stretch without water. But that was enough to know. Thousands would die with the aqueduct water cut off—and their deaths would be excruciating.

Kurt tapped the paper in his hand. "See my list? Every last aqueduct."

And Roberto ran. He just took off.

He ducked this way and that, swerving behind rubble, hoping to dodge the bullets he expected. Instead, a German soldier tackled him from behind and sat on him and pounded him with both fists, till Kurt called the man off.

After that, Kurt tied a rope around Roberto's chest and tied the other end to his own belt. Roberto was on a leash.

They exploded electrical plants and put mines outside the buildings so that fire trucks couldn't come up to put out the flames.

They bombed all the remaining aqueducts.

They shot anyone who protested—man or woman. Shot them. Dead.

Roberto was dragged through it all.

Then Kurt finally found a use for Roberto. He had him spread the news: every Italian man between eighteen and thirty-three years old was to report for work by September 25. They'd be forced labor for the Germans. Roberto knew all about forced labor—that's how he'd become part of this whole damnable war in the first place. He shouted the announcement over and over till he was hoarse.

But the twenty-fifth came and only 150 men had reported for work, out of the tens of thousands who had to be eligible. Scholl was apoplectic. Something unspeakable was bound to happen. Roberto felt the danger like an electrical current racing through his limbs. At any given moment he was holding in a scream.

Kurt and his soldiers stamped through the streets and forced doors. When doors wouldn't open, they shot out the locks. If there were no men in the house, the women were questioned, and if the Germans didn't believe them, they shot them. If there were men and if they had guns, they shot them. They shot parents while children looked on. And Roberto stood there, arms tied behind his back, tethered to Kurt, and saw it all. His mouth was the conduit for every evil word. He wanted to bite his own tongue off.

Some men came out with their hands up. A few had ID cards, showing they were members of the Italian Fascist party; they were on the Germans' side. They should be let free.

But the ID cards made no difference. All the men were gathered and marched out of town. One asked where they were going. He was shot. A boy tried to run away. He was shot. They marched for hours, all afternoon, all night. Women who offered them water along the road were beaten.

Kurt and Roberto marched behind them. Hour after hour. Ten hours. Eleven hours. Finally they stopped and built a fire against the late September chill.

Roberto was exhausted, and it felt good. He was beyond tension, beyond the fear that had squeezed him for so long. His body was nothing but a limp sack of organs.

The Germans huddled together, muttering. The trucks that were supposed to meet them weren't coming after all. Messages hadn't gotten through, because wires were down. So at dawn, they marched all the men back to Naples.

Roberto spent the next days tied to the leg of the piano in the hotel headquarters lobby while Scholl tried to figure out what to do next.

The Germans talked of street urchins—those boys in shorts—those boys like Roberto. The boys were stealing gasoline and arms, even automatic rifles. Ordinary men were picking up shovels and pitchforks and hammers and bricks. They fought off soldiers who came to their houses.

Scholl and his men made fun of them: "Orphans and bumpkins." But look what the orphans and bumpkins were doing! Roberto cheered for them inside his head. He cheered when they destroyed German tanks. He cheered when they stopped Nazis from blowing up a bridge.

Kurt spluttered, "Stupid Neapolitans. Disorganized—no plan of attack—just a bunch of separate little ambushes. They can't really do us damage."

But Scholl shook his head. He said they needed a show of force to put down the rebellions long enough for the Germans to get out of town and away.

So the Germans took hostages. Men, women, and eleven children. They announced they'd kill them—all of them—if the Italians didn't let them leave town unhindered.

The leader of the Neapolitan rebels came to German headquarters to negotiate. He met with Colonel Scholl by candlelight, because the Germans had destroyed the utility plant.

The rebel leader looked like nothing more than an overgrown street urchin himself. But he spoke with power. He said the Germans had to let the hostages go or the rebels would fight till every last German was dead. He said it like a crazy man; his voice shook. And Roberto translated with all the maniacal fury he could muster. In that moment, Roberto shared the power.

Colonel Scholl let the hostages go.

The Germans drove out of town in their trucks.

With Roberto, the point of a gun pressed against the small of his back.

· 9 ·

THE NIGHT AIR MADE ROBERTO SHIVER. He still wore only shorts. He wished he could at least rub his arms, but his wrists remained tied behind him.

Dark had come early, and maneuvering around the mess of crumpled walls in the streets of Naples had taken a long time. But now, on the open road, the trucks went fast and the breeze they created chilled. There was one good thing about that, though: it carried away the smoke from Kurt's cigar, so Roberto didn't have to fight off a gag.

And the rope around his chest was gone. Another thing to be grateful for.

After a few hours, the truck convoy stopped by the side of the road. Roberto walked into the bushes with the soldiers to relieve himself. He waited for Kurt to untie his wrists.

Shots came.

The soldier beside Roberto fell face forward.

Roberto had no idea where the bullets came from, so he

didn't know which way to run. He dropped to his knees and let himself fall on his side, to get out of the gun's line of sight.

Something gushed from the mouth of the shot soldier. He gurgled. His eyes opened and closed, opened and closed.

More shots. Now from lots of directions.

Kurt stumbled past, screaming, his hands clutching the back of his neck. He disappeared in the bushes.

More shots. Germans shouting and running. The engine noises from the trucks. Then nothing.

The dying soldier beside Roberto coughed and choked and went silent.

Again. Roberto had found himself in the middle of death again. Again and again and again. Death stained every place he went. Every place for the past year and a half. Death and death. How could it keep happening, over and over and over? It should be done. Over and done.

He should be dead.

The thought was iron-heavy with its truth. What made him so special that he kept getting away? Nothing. Roberto wasn't special at all. He was an ordinary person. A kid. He was supposed to be dead by now.

From here to Venice, Italy was occupied with Germans. He'd never make it home.

And right now he couldn't even remember home.

A vast sense of failure pinned him to the ground.

Soon whispers came. In some southern Italian dialect. Roberto didn't try to make out what the people were saying to each other. He didn't care.

Quiet footsteps came close. Something tapped him on the shoulder. Then a face stared into his. A boy's face. A teen. "You're alive." He put a pistol to Roberto's forehead. "Beg. Beg like you Nazis made my father beg before you shot him. Beg, so I can shoot you."

"I don't want to beg," said Roberto. "I don't want anything."

"Italian, huh?" The boy moved the pistol down to Roberto's throat. "So you're a Fascist, not a Nazi. That's worse. You're the lowest of the low."

"I'm not a Fascist."

"Oh no? Who are you?"

Roberto closed his eyes. "No one."

There was the sound of running from behind Roberto. "I can't find anyone else alive," said a second voice, breathy and excited. It was just a kid's, too. "We took out four of them, at least. Who's this?"

"No One."

"Why are his hands tied?"

"His hands are tied? Oh yeah? Open your eyes, boy."

The pistol was still touching Roberto's throat. He opened his eyes.

"What were you doing with the Germans?"

"Translating."

"You speak German? How'd you learn it?"

"I was with Samuele—"

"A Jew? You were with a Jew?"

"He was my best friend. We were in a work camp." That was so long ago. Over a year ago. It felt like forever. And that wasn't where Roberto had learned the language, anyway. Roberto was too exhausted to say it all. "It's hard to explain."

"We know about work camps. The Nazis took lots of men from around here and forced them to go to Germany to work camps. But they didn't take boys."

"They took me," said Roberto. "I keep getting taken by the Germans. It's happened three times now."

The first boy shook the gun in front of Roberto's eyes. "Stand up."

Roberto got to his feet. Now he took a look at the second boy; that boy carried a shovel in each hand. These two boys had ambushed a German truck convoy. Alone. What gall. Like the orphan rebels against the Germans in Naples. No, even more exaggerated than that. Like David against Goliath.

"Turn around."

Why? But who cared why? Roberto turned around.

The boy cut the rope from his wrists.

"So, No One, do you know, is there anyone else alive here?"

Was Kurt still alive? He'd gone off somewhere in the

bushes ahead. But Roberto owed him, for shooting the boy back in the piazza in Naples. Shooting him so he didn't have to burn up in the fire. He crossed his arms over his cold chest and rubbed his shoulders and upper arms. "No."

"You cold?" asked the second boy.

"Yeah."

"Want that German's shirt?" He kicked the boot of the dead man beside Roberto.

"No."

"All right, then."

The boys gathered the guns and ammunition from the dead. Then each took a shovel and dug a shallow grave. They rolled the dead soldier into it and covered him up. Then they did the same to the three other dead soldiers.

They walked along the paved road a way and then turned up a dirt path. No one talked. They came to a wide pine and brushed away needles at the foot of it to expose a metal trunk. They stashed the guns and ammunition there. All but the older boy's pistol. Then they continued up the road. They came to a peasant house in the middle of farmland.

The main room of the home had a stone-flagged floor. A carbide lamp hissed gently over a table. Salami and garlic and onions hung from roof rafters in the corner.

A woman came through one of the doorways. She saw Roberto and clapped her hands together and shook them at the boys in exasperation. "What have you brought me?"

"He was a prisoner of the Germans."

"You went near the Germans again? Are you crazy? Will you never get any sense into your thick skulls?" She rushed over and smacked the older boy on the back of the head. Then she smacked the younger one. "You think you know what you're dealing with. But you don't."

She put her hands to her mouth now and tilted her head toward Roberto, and her eyes looked so sad. "Where do you belong, boy?" Her words were kind, as though this was a normal world where adults worried about the sense in their sons' skulls and people cared about the fate of a lost boy. She spoke like anyone's mother anywhere.

It was too normal to bear.

Roberto stood there and cried.

·10·

ROBERTO LAY IN THE GRASS. The ground beside him moved. A mole burrowed up, saw him, and disappeared under again. A jay screamed and screamed in the nearest willow tree. Roberto got up and looked. A snake dropped from the yellowing leaves.

Evening was coming fast. And night here was dark.

That was a good thing about this place. The darkness of the night. At night in Venice the moon reflects off the water. And everywhere he'd been since, the night had somehow glowed. Off the snow, off the water. But here the moon and stars were absorbed by the fields. Night was black. The newness of that offered relief from any chance of memory.

He would have liked to sleep outside in that blackness. But Rina, the mother of this family, wouldn't hear of it. She made him sleep on a mattress stuffed with corncobs—the same kind everyone else in the family slept on. Roberto's was old and pressed thin with wear. It had been discarded but not yet burned, lucky for him. Rina placed it in the barn, with the oxen.

Roberto walked between a willow and a poplar, part of a line of trees connected by vines, which formed a natural fence between the fields. The other workers had gone back to the farmhouse a while ago to clean up before dinner. But Roberto had formed the habit of lagging behind. No one seemed to mind, so long as he showed up for the meal.

Maybe he'd lagged a bit too long today, though. He hurried now, straight to the well. Two copper pitchers were waiting on the ground beside it. He filled them, like usual, then carried one in each hand. He hardly felt the dig of the thin metal handles anymore, his hands had already grown hard from cutting maize stalks all day.

He wore old trousers, a shirt without a collar, and a jacket without sleeves. Rina had pulled them from a trunk for him. They fit okay.

Planes went by overhead. Roberto could tell from the sound that there were several of them. He didn't look up.

When he got to the house, the thick smell of minestra greeted him, cabbage rich. He'd come to love Rina's minestra. He put the pitchers on the sideboard and washed his hands and face in the basin with the water the boys had already used for the same purpose. Then he helped set the table. The boys didn't help in that kind of work. But Roberto liked doing it. Their teasing didn't bother him. And he knew it made Rina feel better about having him around—about having one more mouth to feed.

Rina put two hot loaves of bread on the table, and the boys appeared as if by magic. Four of them. The two who had found Roberto that night in the bushes: Ivano, the one with the gun, and Angelo. Plus Manfreddo, who was older, and Emilio, who was a lot younger. They were brothers—Rina's children.

Roberto picked up a long loaf and held it upright to his chest. Its warmth felt wonderful through his jacket. He cut it into wedges, drawing the knife toward his chest. He'd learned that way of cutting bread from the oldest brother. It felt honest to hug the bread like that—respectful acknowledgment of how essential it was. He wished he could give a loaf like this to every fourteen-year-old girl in Naples. His eyes burned for an instant.

The boys dropped pieces of bread into their bowls of minestra and ate greedily, talking about the grape harvest that would start in the morning. Roberto listened only enough to get an idea of what his next job would be. They had harvested about half the grapes before he got there, using some for eating and the rest for wine. But the other half were still on the vine. The blush of maturity had passed. The grapes were partly dry. It didn't make any sense to Roberto. But, then, not much made sense to him. He was a city boy. Venice didn't have fields to work. Or not on the main islands, anyway. His only experience with field labor before now was that afternoon he'd spent cutting and rolling wheat with the two little boys in Sicily. He ate the cheese and nuts and grapes that followed the soup without hearing anything really.

After dinner everyone went outside to relieve themselves in the outhouse. Though the farmhouse had electricity, it had no running water and no bathroom. Then the boys went inside to gather around the radio, while Rina washed the dishes in the water Roberto had brought from the well. Roberto went to the barn. He couldn't bear listening to war news on the radio. He didn't care about battles anywhere.

Venice was occupied by the Nazis. His Venice. His parents. So long as that was true, he couldn't go home. Rina said it was too dangerous.

After all that Roberto had been through, it was almost laughable how he obeyed the warnings of this mild woman. But he did. It felt good to be treated like a child by her.

And obeying her gave him the excuse he needed. He didn't want to leave this farm. He wished he was home with his family, oh, Lord, how he wished that. But he couldn't travel there; he couldn't bear the thought of meeting up with German soldiers again. Soon enough the Allies would take back the north of Italy from Hitler, and then he'd leave. Only then. He'd go to Venice. But for now, he was where he had to be. He was staying put.

Tonight shouts came from the house. Roberto was leaning over the half-door of the oxen stable, surprised at how he could pick out the white one from the brindled gray and brown one in the dark. He heard the shouts but didn't turn around. He reached out and ran his hand down the length of one long horn and up the length of the next. He was careful to keep his arm away from the mucus that dripped almost continually from the ox's muzzle.

"We did it." Ivano's voice came strong and happy behind Roberto. "We declared war on Germany. Finally. October 13 is the best day of my life."

"We've been at war with Germany, maybe all along," said Roberto, turning around.

"Not officially. Yesterday the Americans secured Naples. They'll take Rome next week. No doubt about it. And I'm going to be part of it."

Roberto's cheeks felt heavy. "What do you mean?"

"I'm joining the *partigiani*—the resistance fighters. I'll go behind the enemy lines into occupied Italy. I'll kill those Nazis. With their own pistol."

Their own pistol. So that pistol Ivano had was from a German. Did he get it the same way he got the guns and ammunition that were hidden in the metal trunk? There was a time when Roberto had never seen a real gun. The police in Venice didn't carry them. But for so long now, guns had surrounded him. Guns and grenades and bombs.

"I'll go all the way to Venice," said Ivano.

Roberto wished he could see Ivano's eyes in the dark of the barn—the bright wetness of them. He had the eerie sensation of talking to a disembodied voice, the voice of a dead man. "Does your mother know?"

"No. I won't tell her. I'll help with the grapes and the wine. Then I'll just leave."

Roberto wanted to say, Don't. Don't do that to your mother. But he knew Ivano by now. There was no point. He turned back to the oxen.

"All the way to Venice. Your city." Ivano came up beside him and rested his forearms on the top of the stable half-door. "Come with me."

Back into the middle of war.

Roberto had once planned to join the *partigiani*. He and Maurizio were going to do it together. Like brothers. Maurizio would have made a terrific big brother. Roberto squeezed his eyes shut for an instant—*please please let his real big brother be alive still. Let Sergio be fine.*

"You know you want to. Come on, Roberto."

"No."

"You have almost as much reason to hate them as I do."

Hate? Roberto felt too tired to even think about hate.

Ivano left.

Roberto lay down on his mattress. The oxen chewed. Their bellies rumbled. Their dung fell with a splash. Hour after hour he listened to them shifting their massive weight.

· 11 ·

Roberto woke to dawn air, warm from oxen breath. Breakfast was the remains of last night's bread broken into bowls of warm buffalo milk with sugar. Today they would pick the lightly shriveled grapes, sometimes one by one, and drop them into the handcart.

Angelo said picking grapes earlier in the season was easy compared to this—you just ripped off the whole bunch, stems and all. He smiled. "It's worth it, though. The wine from these grapes, ah, it tastes like honey and oranges. It's spicy. It deserves to be called holy."

They picked all day long. Roberto had no time at the end of the day to lie in the grasses. But boys from neighboring farms had come to help, so at least they finished the harvesting. Women Roberto didn't know joined Rina in spreading out the grapes on straw mats to dry even more.

After dinner, Ivano and Angelo came into the barn. "Get up," said Angelo.

Roberto got up and followed them around the little pond. Geese hissed at them. The boys had never led Roberto anywhere at night before. Still, he was neither afraid nor excited. His only thought was that he didn't want to get too close to those geese.

The boys walked in such a tight band that they could smell one another's hair and hear one another's breath. They walked a long while, then climbed a hill and sat in a row. Ivano pointed.

Lights. Headlights. Roberto could make out the black snake of a road way down there. Now he saw a second set of headlights.

"Nazi trucks," said Angelo.

"I'm going to blow up trucks just like those," said Ivano. "See that?"

A third set of headlights came along the road, smaller ones, closer together.

"That's a staff car. Officers are in it. If it were daytime, you'd see the mottled camouflage. I'll blow up staff cars, too."

Nazis. Trucks and staff cars and airplanes. Somewhere out there a war was still going on. And Ivano wanted to be part of it. Ivano and Angelo had killed four German soldiers. Maybe they'd killed others, too, before that ambush of the convoy that Roberto was in. He didn't know. But four was enough. Four was too many.

Roberto put his chin on his knees and stared through the air, out over the treetops into nowhere.

Two days later they made wine. Roberto climbed into the vat when it was his turn. His scrubbed feet sank into the pulp, all the way up to his knees. He stamped, lifting his knees high and coming down as hard as he could on the toughened grape skins. The remaining pips and stray stalks resisted. The juice was thick between his toes, sticky like blood. A trough sloped out of the bottom edge of the vat, and juice ran into a bucket. The bucket filled fast. Then one of the boys turned the spigot off and put his hand under it for security while another boy took away the full bucket and a third boy put an empty bucket in place. Now and then a boy put his mouth on the spigot and let the juice run right in. Usually it squirted up his nose and all over his face, as well.

The buckets were emptied into a wooden vat in the back of the cellar. It was so tall, there was barely enough room between the top and the ceiling to turn over a bucket.

Like before, the work took all day long, with no time for lying in the grass at the end. That was all right with Roberto. Exhaustion was a welcome thing.

That night Ivano came into the barn again. "You should have listened to the radio tonight."

"I don't want to know about the war," said Roberto.

"You're the one who had a Jewish friend."

Roberto pushed himself up to sitting. "What happened?"

"The Nazis sprayed bullets over the Jewish ghetto in Rome today. And they arrested more than a thousand people. They're going to send them by train to Germany and Poland."

Roberto put his hands on top of his head and dropped his chin to his chest. He knew about the death camps in Germany and Poland. He wanted to scream at Ivano to stop talking.

But he didn't have to. Ivano left.

A few days later Angelo brought Roberto into the cellar to put his ear to the vat. It rumbled. Angelo smiled. "It's working."

They skimmed off the impurities that had risen to the top of the vats. Clouds of tiny red-headed flies circled there. The air was alcohol. They squeezed the rubbish and put the solids into the slop jar for the pigs. They saved the liquid, and the next day they mixed it with water and drank it in the middle of the day. Rina called it *mezz' vin*—half wine.

Life on this farm was continual toil. Blessed toil from Roberto's point of view; work kept thoughts at bay. The only one who didn't have to work was Emilio. He was ten. Rina said that when he turned twelve he'd work like the rest of them. Till then, she spoiled him. It was a good system. Ten was little. Roberto could hardly remember being ten, but he could tell from Emilio's smile how little ten was.

Roberto helped Rina spoil the boy. He became an expert at making the pancakes Emilio loved. He warmed the special tongs in the fireplace. Then he brushed them with oil and dipped them, hot, into the bowl of batter. He pressed the two sides together. Little bits of batter sizzled out at the sides. He opened the tongs and dropped the pancake right into Emilio's hands. The boy ate it with soft cheese. Then a second and a third and a fourth, before they even called in the other brothers for their share of the treat.

Less than a week after picking the grapes for that wine, Ivano disappeared. Rina pressed her forehead against the doorframe and sobbed. Her fingers curled around the frame. Her body seemed to collapse in on itself.

After that, Roberto worked doubly hard. Especially since Angelo wasn't working anymore—because he had to go back to school. Roberto was needed on this farm now, truly needed. He took over the job of mucking out the hog barn, even though the mean pigs scared him and the stench turned his stomach.

And he joined the others around the radio at night. But there was no news of Allied progress in taking Italy back from the Nazis. Nothing. What were the Allies doing? Why weren't they helping Italy?

Weeks went by. Months. In November the Jews in Florence and Bologna were deported. In December the Jews in Milan, Verona, and Trieste were deported. Children were doubled up in classrooms to free up whole schools as prisons for Jews. When that wasn't enough, abandoned castles served as prisons. Jews' belongings were sequestered. And the Vatican said nothing—as Rina put it, "The pope sits on his hands."

All this time, and Ivano still didn't come back. Christmas and New Year's came and went. Rina sent the boys out in the bitter cold to ask everyone they knew for news of Ivano. The harshest winter Italy had seen in decades drew to a close. And still no word. And still Rome was occupied by the Germans. And still everything north of Rome—including Roberto's beloved Venice—belonged to the Germans. And still Jews were being deported, three thousand of them, four thousand, five.

No word from Ivano. Nothing nothing nothing.

The Allies didn't come and didn't come and didn't come.

The Jews were rotting who knew where.

Italy was occupied.

The war went on.

·12·

PLOUGHING IN THE RAIN WAS HARD. Roberto and Manfreddo and Angelo screamed at the oxen to make them move. The boys tugged at the nose rings. Their feet slipped in the mire. The oxen didn't budge. It was as though they'd formed a pact between them. Their breath made hot clouds around the boys. Their tracks—like huge swallows without tails—puddled with cold rain.

"Eat," called Rina. She stood at the edge of the field with an umbrella in one hand and a basket in the other. Usually on a Sunday like this, the only day when school wasn't in session, Emilio would be at her side, holding a basin of water for them to rinse their face and hands in—but not today. It was raining too hard today.

The boys wiped their hands on their trousers, then held them up to the rain to finish cleaning them. They ran to Rina and unwrapped the cloth in the basket to find hot pizza—thick dough, flavored with the earliest spring onions. They gnawed on hard cheese between bites of that pizza. They drank wine thinned with water. It was so good to eat—so good. When your belly was empty and your arms and back ached from work, nothing was better than pizza.

Manfreddo watched Roberto and Angelo eating. "Look, it's raining too hard to get those lazy oxen moving. Angelo, you unhitch them and let them wander back to the barn. Then rub them down and clean off the plough and put it away before you come out again. Roberto and I will finally work the hill field. The oxen are no use there anyway."

It sounded to Roberto as though Angelo was getting the harder task. Dragging that plough back to the barn in this mud would take so much strength. But he followed Manfreddo obediently to the barn and accepted the hoe he was handed. It had a blade as long as his forearm.

They walked to the sloping field, the only one that hadn't yet been touched this spring. Manfreddo swung his hoe and slammed it into the wet earth. It came up caked with clay. He swung again and again. After every five digs, he wiped off the clay.

Roberto mimicked him. But he quickly found that he had to wipe his blade after every other swing. Otherwise the clay clinging to the blade made it too heavy for him. In minutes, he was covered with sweat despite that cold rain. This was bitterly hard work.

Spring.

Spring in Venice was birdsong and a return to playing in the sand on the beach island—the Lido—and lots of sparkling sun on the water.

Spring on this farm was work. Oh, the birds came, too. Shy jays in pink and black with flashes of white and blue on their wings. Green woodpeckers and wagtails over by the stream. Hawks above the meadows. And the night was full of the delight of fireflies. But mostly spring meant work.

That was good, though. Every part of Roberto's body had been strong in the autumn from all the farmwork. Winter had softened him a little. Now he was getting strong again. This was good. And the rain meant the earth would be ready for planting. This was what a farm was all about. He swung his hoe rhythmically: swing, swing, wipe; swing, swing, wipe.

The work filled his brain. It overflowed. There wasn't room for thought. Nothing existed in the world but this earth, this hoe. But, then, he hit a stone. A gray stone. Flat on one side and rounded on the other. He picked it up.

A Jewish girl had given him a stone like this one in Poland so long ago. He tossed it away. He wouldn't think about it.

Swing swing wipe.

But that one memory was like the single shot at the start of a battle; memories rushed him, things he'd promised himself he'd never think about again.

It was almost two years ago, June 1942. Roberto was in a

movie theater. A normal day. Normal kids at the movies. Then Nazi Secret Service soldiers marched down the aisles and gathered all the boys. They forced them onto trains going north into Germany. Without even telling anyone. Roberto and his brother and his friends—all kidnapped.

He was separated from his brother early on, and he prayed Sergio had made it home. Otherwise his parents might still have no idea what had happened to their children. That thought drove Roberto crazy sometimes—that image of Mamma crying in the circle of Papà's arms.

Swing, swing, wipe.

Roberto and his friend Samuele were sent to a work camp near Munich. They built tarmacs and loaded planes. Then they got moved to Poland and built barbed-wire pens—like the one the Polish girl was imprisoned in. Roberto remembered her bone-thin arms, the little girl that clung to her, the food he sneaked them both, the stone she'd given him in return. A gift. A talisman.

Swing, swing, wipe.

They moved on to a work camp in Ukraine, where the snow made the German soldiers shiver as hard as the Italian boys. Where Samuele died, protecting Roberto's shoes from a thief. His friend died. His best friend. And Roberto had had enough. He walked away, expecting to be shot in the back by the Nazi soldiers in charge of the boys.

Instead, he tramped through snow for days, got shot and

captured by Ukrainians, escaped, and made it down the river in a boat he'd found under a bush. That's where he'd met up, by chance, with Maurizio, the Roman deserter, who saved him from the infection in his bullet wound.

Swing, swing, wipe.

Maurizio told him about the *partigiani*. They vowed that when they got home, they'd join up and help sabotage the war; Hitler had to be stopped.

Swing, swing, wipe.

They went in that small boat along the coast of the Black Sea, and cut across the narrow passageway through Turkey into the Mediterranean. That's where villagers got the better of them. They were stupid enough to think a fisherman had overlooked squid eggs in his cast-aside net. While they were busy eating the eggs, the villagers stole their boat. It was easy to get tricked when they were so hungry they'd been chomping on pine needles, as though a jaw could be fooled simply by the act of chewing. Maurizio had mumbled, "A couple of cows, chewing our cud." And he laughed. His laugh used to make Roberto feel almost happy.

Swing, swing, wipe.

Walking home would have been impossible; it would have taken months, and they were hungry. So they pirated away a sailboat and its Turkish captain. No, that made it sound romantic. What they did was steal; they stole the boat. Roberto didn't want to. He was a Venetian—and in Venice no one was lower than a boat thief. But it was a big, rich boat. Like the ones he'd watched wealthy Americans sun themselves on in Venice before the war. That wasn't as bad as stealing a fishing boat, someone's livelihood. It wasn't.

Roberto had never before been so far out at sea. In every direction indigo water met cerulean sky, with sun dazzling dazzling, like the world was ready to flicker into flames at the first rasping wind. He loved it.

He remembered looking down off the side of the yacht at light glancing off a reddish brown oval just under the surface. And there was a second one. And a third. Lots of them. Turtles! They darted around and under the boat, their strong fins making them soar, so that Roberto half expected them to leap into the air. He laughed.

He was happy then, not almost, but really. The captain had agreed, under duress, to take them to Italy. These turtles were their escort.

But the captain delivered them, instead, into the hands of a German ship off Crete. Captured by the Germans again.

Maybe that's what a boat thief deserved.

Swing, swing, wipe.

The German officer at the base on Suda Bay spoke Italian. He looked at the stuff from their pockets—a knife and compass from Maurizio's, the Polish girl's stone from Roberto's. He called them spies and put them in separate corners and grilled them. When they wouldn't speak, he said they were deserters, and he'd shoot them.

Roberto clutched at the chair he sat on. That couldn't be. You don't shoot prisoners. You put them behind bars. You don't shoot them. No one shoots them.

The commander barked an order in German.

"Wait," said Maurizio. "Roberto's a child. You can't kill—"

They shot him midsentence.

"Maurizio!" Roberto ran toward his friend, but he fell, pushed from behind. His teeth smacked on the floor.

A black boot rolled him onto his back. "If you had come yesterday, I'd have greeted you with a Happy New Year celebration," said the commander. "But gunshots a day late aren't so bad, eh?" He picked up the stone and slammed Maurizio's head with it. The Polish girl's gift stone.

It didn't matter, Roberto told himself, it didn't matter, because Maurizio was already dead. The blood on the stone glistened in the sunlight. The commander threw it out the window.

Swing, swing, wipe.

No one deserved that. Not even a boat thief.

Swing, swing, wipe.

Swing, swing, wipe.

They put him to work in the kitchen. Without realizing he was doing it, Roberto became an eavesdropper. He knew a little German from the work camps, and one day he found he'd somehow absorbed enough German so that he could get the gist of what was said. The German soldiers talked about battles. Roberto hated it. He was on no one's side. He must have been crazy to have ever thought he could join the *partigiani*. Maurizio was a soldier—he had the heart of a hero. But Roberto couldn't shoot a gun. He wouldn't. He hated war.

Spring came to Crete, and somewhere in there his birthday passed. Then one day the German ships loaded up and went to fight the Americans and the British in North Africa. They took Roberto to his first battle.

Swing, swing, wipe.

Roberto's head throbbed. Memories were bullets.

Swing, swing, wipe.

Crack! He was underwater. He swam hard for the surface, bursting out at the last moment. His whole body sucked in air. Pieces of metal and rope and rubber splashed down around him. His ship had been hit.

Roberto swam for open water, swam for hours. Sometime in the night he washed up onshore far from the harbor, like a dead thing. Joe and Randy, some American soldiers, found him. They couldn't believe a kid his age was off alone in the middle of a war. They offered him a smoke. When he didn't take the cigarette, they gave him a chocolate bar. "Hershey's," Joe said. They watched him eat and lick his fingers, and they laughed.

He patrolled the coast with them. They slept in shallow trenches in the sand. They ate straight from cans. The pears were delicious, in their thick syrup. And Randy taught Roberto the names of all the birds in English. So many birds.

At night Roberto watched the wave crests break into glowing white sea foam. At dawn he watched flamingos ascend in huge, rosy clouds.

That week was like a dream.

But the next was a nightmare. They were called to Lake Bizerte to help process Axis prisoners from a huge battle there. Joe, who spoke broken Italian, told Roberto to keep his mouth shut. If anyone knew he was Italian, he'd be taken prisoner, too.

Bizerte was a mess. The buildings had been smashed by heavy shelling, the streets blown to dust. Arabs draped in white cloths watched them walk by, their faces as immobile as those of the camels that stood beside them, held by a halter. One little girl peeked out from around a man, looked at Roberto, and ran her fingers across her throat, as though she were slashing it. Her eyes flashed hatred. Stray dogs and cats skittered out of their way.

And then they got to the prisoners. Most were German. The rest, Italian. Prisoners and prisoners and prisoners. They stretched off in lines as far as Roberto could see.

The Italian soldiers' feet bled; Mussolini didn't provide shoes. Their rolled-up pants and unbuttoned shirts revealed scabs and bruises. They talked about how being captured was the best thing that could have happened. They swarmed gratefully into cages made of barbed wire and cactus hedges, and held out their hands for cans of beef and packets of biscuits. They ate like the starving.

A German band of seven motley performers played music through it all. Some Axis soldiers actually swung their fingers in the air in time with the beat. One man swung an arm missing its hand. The worst sight, though, was the dead. Floating, bloated bodies filled Lake Bizerte.

The infantry prisoners walked to their cages. But the Nazi officers climbed into jeeps or their own little staff cars and actually drove themselves to prison, swerving around the corpses. And the vultures.

Abandoned tanks. Shovels, pipes, shattered guns, empty helmets. Twisted telegraph wires. Piles of burnt, blackened things—charred beyond recognition.

At one point a shell came tearing out of nowhere. Everyone jumped and aimed their guns. But it had just come from a pile of flaming debris.

Bodies sank into the soft ground, as though part of the earth itself. American soldiers turned them over with their boots, looking for the living. Swarms of flies rose and settled again. The Americans chewed gum and moved on.

The pungent smell of burning—oil and steel and cloth—

welled up everywhere. And dust. Soldiers wrapped cloth around their faces to keep it out. It didn't work.

After Bizerte, Joe and Randy and Roberto climbed into a truck and went west with other Allied soldiers, across Tunisia into Algeria. They passed dummies in Allied uniforms, stuffed with dried grasses and topped with helmets, made up to look like antitank gun crews from above, to lure Axis planes into wasting bombs on them.

In Algeria they trained for the invasion of Sicily. Then they got into the Landing Ship Tanks and went across the sea. The whole way the soldiers talked about land mines and how many people they'd seen have a leg blown off, or an arm, or a head. After a while Joe stopped translating for Roberto.

It was just as well.

Swing, swing, wipe.

·13·

THAT EVENING RINA FED THEM CALF'S BOWEL—long lengths of boiled hose—with beans and wild greens. For dessert they had cheese and the last of the dried pears. It might rain its heart out outside, but in this house there was warmth.

They had settled around the radio when the knock came. Manfreddo opened the door.

A small person came in, hunched over in a drenched coat. From the shoes, Roberto knew immediately this was a girl. So did Rina. She stopped washing the dishes and rushed to help the girl out of her long, dripping coat. "Come, sit. Have you eaten?"

The girl's face was round, like a child's, but inside that worn cotton dress she was clearly a young woman. And her eyes were huge and sunken with sadness. She reached a hand down the neck of her dress and pulled out an envelope.

Rina sat at the table. The lamp hissed. No one spoke.

The girl put the envelope on the table in front of Rina. Her arms were skinny. Her hands struck Roberto as too tiny to be useful.

Roberto filled a bowl from the pot of beans and bowels that was still sitting on the woodstove. He put it on the table.

Manfreddo had been staring at the envelope. But now he seemed to wake up. "Sit," he said to the girl, gesturing toward the bowl, awkward in the role of host but trying his best. "Please eat a little."

The girl sat. She took a bite. Then she ate steadily. Roberto sensed she was working not to rush, not to seem rude. He recognized the struggle; this girl was very hungry.

Rina spoke with her eyes on the envelope. "Forgive us for being so inhospitable. We didn't even introduce ourselves."

"I know who you are," said the girl. She stopped eating and put her hands in her lap. "It is an honor to meet you finally, Signora Coeli." She bowed her head to Rina. Then she looked at the boys. "And to meet you, Manfreddo . . ." She stood and held out her hand across the table. Manfreddo shook it. She studied the other boys. ". . . and Angelo . . . and Emilio . . . and Roberto." She shook hands with each of them after she said their name; she picked the right boy for each name. "I am Teresa." She sat again.

Rina opened the envelope. It was a letter. Emilio went over and stood by her shoulder. Rina gasped.

"Come here," said Manfreddo to Emilio. He gathered his

youngest brother under one arm and Angelo under the other. He looked at Roberto. "Get over here." Roberto moved close to Emilio's other side. They huddled, their eyes on Rina's face.

Rina's mouth moved as she read silently. Her eyes brimmed with tears. Then she put the letter down and sobbed. The others circled her, everyone hugging, everyone crying, even Teresa.

Then Rina pushed them all away. She went into her little room. She shut the door.

Manfreddo picked up the letter. He read aloud.

VIA REINA, 5
MILAN 12 MARCH 1944

My dear mamma and brothers,

I write to you from prison. The German Military Tribunal has condemned me—General Kesselring has signed the sentence. I'll die this evening. They'll shoot me.

I know I should have written to you sooner. I thought about you often. But I was busy. And asking someone to carry a message home would only have taken one more person out of the good fight for the length of the journey.

Know that I fought well.

At first I fought for revenge. Because of Papà. Because of how the Nazis shot him down for doing nothing but standing by the side of the road as they passed.

But then I learned what this war is about. And when I found out, I thought I was losing my mind. This is a war about the most basic things. About freedom. And dignity. Every ugly thing you hear about the Fascists and the Nazis is true. Every ugly thing you've ever imagined happens under their guard. And things you'd never ever be able to imagine on your own—they happen, too.

They say that if they shoot enough of us, they'll kill the spirits of the rest of us. They'll triumph. But that's wrong. All of us who know the truth about this war—we are like the spine of a giant animal, a wild thing that can never be tamed, never be caught in a cage. We will carry that beast forever, to victory. One after the other of us. No matter what.

But, really, I don't think the Nazis even believe that shooting us will stop the resistance. They shoot us just to make terror—just to do as much harm as they can before the end. Because they know they will lose in the end. They have to.

Can you believe I am writing this way? Me, who never even liked school. Now I wish I had paid attention in history lessons.

Angelo and Emilio, study well at school. Do better than me. There's a lot to learn.

Manfreddo, take care of Mamma. But don't forget to make your own family. I have been lucky. I have loved Volpe Rossa—red fox. I wish you love, too.

And, Mamma, please know that I fought well. My heart is at peace now, because I know I did my duty as a son and an Italian. I have come to cherish my ideals, conscious that I might have to give everything for them, even my life. This was my decision. I die with the calm of the strong. Know this. You can lift your chin higher now, for you raised me well. Despite all my foolishness before, despite how you worried, I grew up to be good. Don't cry. And, please, forgive me for the pain that I've caused you. And, Mamma, be happy for me. I die like a man.

I go now to join Papà, the one I have missed so much.

With my last embrace,
Your Ivano

Manfreddo put down the letter and sat on the floor. Emilio sank onto his lap and circled his arms and legs around him. Angelo stood with his hand on Emilio's head. They rocked forward and backward, crying.

Roberto wiped at his tears. "Would you like another bowl?" he asked Teresa.

She shook her head.

"Then come with me to the barn. You can have my mattress."

"No," said Manfreddo. "She can sleep in our room, and we'll come out to the barn."

And so Teresa went into the other bedroom, and the boys went to the barn.

They put Emilio on the mattress, and the three older boys pushed together straw and fell into a heap. But soon enough, Emilio crawled in on top of them.

Roberto's right arm was wet. Emilio had fallen asleep crying. It was March 22. Ivano had been dead for ten days. He'd never grow up. Or maybe he had. That letter seemed grown up.

In another month, Roberto would turn fifteen. And in a month Roberto would have been at this farm for half a year. He'd hidden for half a year.

Ivano was wrong. Not everyone who knew the truth about this war was part of the spine of that giant animal, that noble beast. Roberto knew the truth, and he was doing nothing about it.

Roberto wanted three things. He wanted to stay safe. He wanted to get home. He wanted this war to end. So far he'd put them in that order of priority. Maybe it was time to rearrange his priorities.

Like the orphans of Naples. They'd put ending the war in first place.

Mamma wouldn't want him to die like Ivano had. Papà wouldn't want him to, either. Roberto didn't want to die doing the honorable thing.

But he no longer wanted to live doing the dishonorable thing.

·14·

RINA LOOKED AT TERESA. "Stay at least a few more days."

Teresa helped serve breakfast. "There's work to do."

"For my sake," said Rina. And she put her hands on a chair back and leaned forward and cried. She had been crying on and off since Sunday night. It was now Tuesday morning. Angelo and Emilio had left for school. They didn't want to go, but Rina said they had to. One day home was enough. It would be better for them to go back to their routine. For all of them. They all had to keep moving.

Roberto and Manfreddo were getting ready for a day of ploughing. It hadn't rained on Monday. That meant the earth was soft, but no longer muddy. The best conditions for ploughing. They would probably finish today, if they could just manage to keep their minds on the job. If they didn't let sorrow immobilize them.

Teresa wore her hair in two tight braids. One had fallen

over her shoulder when she put the bowl of hot milk in front of Roberto. Now she lifted the tips of both braids and tied them over the top of her head. "Manfreddo, are there any clothes Angelo has outgrown in this house?"

"What? Sure. Mamma saves everything."

"All right, then." Teresa kissed Rina on the cheek. "One more day. But only if you let me help in the field."

Manfreddo took the long-bladed hoe and went to the field on the slope of the hill. And, so, Roberto found himself beside Teresa, pushing and pulling the oxen. With a hat covering her tied braids, she seemed like one of the brothers. And she worked like one, too. Her strength surprised him. Roberto realized he didn't know anything about her. She had hardly talked since she got here. "Did you grow up on a farm?" he asked.

"You don't want to know."

"Yes, I do."

"The less you know, the less they can get out of you if they torture you."

Who would come to this farm to torture him? Torture seemed a world away from this valley. And there was something missing from Teresa's argument. "What would it matter if I knew about how you grew up?"

"One bit of information here, another there, a third over there—you put them together and you figure out someone's family." Teresa wiped dirt and sweat from her face and looked at Roberto with disgust. "You really don't know squat about this war, do you? If the Germans had found out anything about Gufo's family, they'd have come and burned down the farmhouse. Rina and Manfreddo and Angelo and Emilio—they'd all be dead now. This is true."

Roberto did too know things about this war. More than he wished he knew. But there was no point in arguing. "Gufo?" he said, instead. Who was Gufo? It was such a strange name—it meant "owl."

"Ivano. Many of the *partigiani* have a *nome di guerra*—a war name. The name of an animal, or maybe of a legendary hero, like Orlando, or maybe a natural phenomenon like Terremoto—'earthquake.' It's what you go by, to keep everyone safe."

"Safe? Who's safe in the middle of war?" Roberto said with challenge in his voice.

Teresa lugged at an ox. "We keep one another's spirits safe. As for the body . . . well, it's going to die sooner or later anyway. But we do what we can to protect it. We don't tell what doesn't need to be told."

"Ivano told you his real name."

"Gufo knew I'd die rather than give him up."

And it dawned on Roberto. Of course. "Are you Volpe Rossa—the red fox in his letter?"

"No one outside the *partigiani* knows our war names."

They reached the end of the row. Roberto turned the oxen around, to start the last row of the field. "How do you keep one another's spirits safe?"

Teresa rubbed her throat. Then she opened her mouth and sang,

"Soffia il vento, urla la bufera,
Scarpe rotte, eppur bisogna andar
A conquistare la rossa primavera
Dove sorge il sol dell'avvenir."

"The wind blows hard—the storm howls—shoes are ruined—but still we must keep going." Her voice was neither clear nor in tune. But the words were fingers, closing around Roberto's heart. She sang of conquering the spring, where the sun of the future rises. She sang of every little neighborhood being the home of rebels, every woman helping, stars guiding, hearts and arms strong in the fight. But she didn't stop there. The words painted naked truth: she sang that if death should get you, the *partigiani* would avenge you. She sang that their fate was surely harsh, in the face of the evil they were chasing. And then she sang of the wind ceasing, the storm calming, and the proud *partigiano* going home, with his red flag unfurling, and all of us victorious, free in the end.

Roberto couldn't speak, his heart hurt so much.

"The Garibaldi Brigade in the northwest—up in Piemonte—they sing that. And it spread. Now all of us sing it."

"Sing it again," said Roberto. "Teach me."

That night Roberto took Teresa on a long walk, all the way to the hill that Ivano and Angelo had taken him to last autumn. They stayed for hours. No Nazi trucks passed on the road below. But it didn't matter. Roberto knew they were out there.

"Have you been far north?" asked Roberto.

"I helped organize the biggest strike—the one at the Fiat plant in Turin last spring. We stopped the city's economy, the whole Fascist machine, for a day. And I sounded the sirens to announce the strike. I did it myself." Her voice rang with pride. "The Fascists didn't want the rest of Italy to know how hard we were fighting against the war up north. They squelched all information about the strikes. You probably didn't even hear about it."

Roberto hadn't heard about it, no, but not because of Fascist censorship. He hadn't even been in Italy then. "Have you been to Venice? Are there lots of Germans there?"

"All of northeast Italy is a German stronghold. It's supposed to be under Mussolini's leadership, but he's just a puppet for Hitler."

"I thought Mussolini was in prison."

"You really know nothing. The Nazis broke into that prison way back in September. They set Mussolini up at Salò as the true head of Italy. So now there are two Italys: the republic aligned with the Allies, led by the king and his General Badoglio. And the Fascist dictatorship aligned with the Nazis, led by Mussolini. And both of them are crippled."

Roberto pressed one fist inside the other hand. Salò wasn't far from Venice. "Are there *partigiani* in Venice, too?"

"There are *partigiani* everywhere. You find good people everywhere."

Roberto let himself fall onto his back. A rock dug into his shoulder. "What's a girl doing in the *partigiani*?"

"What a stupid question. Do you know, that song I taught you—about the wind and the *partigiano*—it was written by Felice Cascione, a girl from Liguria."

A girl had felt the deprivations that twisted through that song. Roberto wondered how old she was. Was she the age of the Polish girl who had given him his talisman stone so long ago now? He could hardly breathe. "Why did you join?"

"It doesn't matter. Everyone has a different story. A German soldier shoots two men, and their widows, who never even liked each other before, find they are best friends. They start a little band of resistance. And they meet another woman, whose father was killed, and she bands with them. And another woman who was raped by a Nazi officer, and she bands with them. And the girl who watched her mother get raped. And the girl who watched her brother get arrested and dragged away. Everyone has a personal story. But in the end, they're all the same."

"What do you mean?"

"Italy has nothing, Roberto. No government—at least not to speak of. This winter was so harsh and there was no fuel. In Rome women would wait in line from three to eleven in the morning to get almost nothing—a half kilo of charcoal. No one could stay warm. No one could buy food—there was so little and it cost so much. And the poor *partigiani* hiding in the mountains, they suffered severely—no sweaters, no blankets. You can't imagine." She stopped and dropped her head. She was silent for so long, Roberto thought she was crying. But when she finally spoke again, her voice came strong. "We Italians, we have nothing. So we choose to have something. We choose resistance."

"Resistance. It's so little. It's just an idea."

"Ideas feed you when the food is gone. They keep you strong. And when you align yourself with others who have the same ideas, you grow more than twice as strong. You grow invincible."

"How can you dare to say that?" asked Roberto. "Ivano just died. In prison."

"But free. In every sense that matters, he died free." Her

voice trembled with pride. "He never bent to the will of the invader."

Could Roberto do that? Could he get caught and thrown in prison and never bend his will? "Tell me about prison."

"In prison," said Teresa, "they give you four hundred grams of bread a day. And a bowl of broth. Thin coffee. Your body weakens quickly. Then they start the questions. They want you to rat on all the other *partigiani*, because they can never find us, and we keep sabotaging their efforts. So they need rats. If you don't answer on the first day, they rip off your eyebrows and eyelashes. On the second, they pull out fingernails and toenails. On the third, they burn the bottom of your feet with candles. On the fourth, they put a collar around your neck with electrical current in it. Ten minutes becomes an eternity. If you still don't talk, you're useless. So they let you buy cigarettes—five lire each, if you can get a friend to give you the money—then they shoot you in the back."

Roberto swallowed the lump that had formed in his throat. "The Germans hate us now that we've turned against them."

"But they hated us before," said Teresa. "They've always hated us. The Italians fought beside the Germans at Stalingrad in Russia last year. They lost so many troops—the defeat was overwhelming. And the retreating German Army refused to help the Italians. They took every car, lorry, truck, and abandoned the Italians, wounded, with no transport or food or medical supplies. Nothing. They've always hated us."

Roberto remembered being in Ukraine and seeing troops march past at a distance. He remembered how poorly dressed the Italians were, how poorly equipped. It was true, what Teresa said. What on earth had made Mussolini join with Hitler, when Hitler so clearly hated the Italians? What made men do such wrong things?

"At least the Allies are fighting with us now."

"You say too many stupid things." Teresa brushed something off her arm. "The Allies, the Allies. Look what they've done for Italy. We joined them, and General Badoglio told us the Americans would take over Italy immediately. That war-mongering idiot!" She slapped her hands together and shook them in front of her face. "Look how far they've come. To Naples—last October. Nothing since. We are occupied—we are being tortured and killed day by day. And the Allies don't give a damn. Why should they? We changed sides in the war; no one trusts us now. No, Roberto, Italy is on her own. The *partigiani* work alone. If Italy is to have a future, it's our job to build it—us, the youth of this country—it's our duty."

"What sort of things do you do?" asked Roberto.

"Anything."

"Like what? What do you, specifically you, do?"

"Not as much as I could if I spoke more German," said Teresa. "I'm lousy at languages."

"You're not answering me."

"Most women work mainly from homes. I do that sometimes. But I go out into the hills, too." She put both hands behind her neck and stretched, her elbows pointing up at the moon for an instant. "Look, Roberto, we just do. We do anything we can to sabotage the German war effort."

Anything? Had Teresa ever picked up a gun? Had anyone pointed a gun at her? Roberto sat up and circled his arms around his knees. "I never want to kill anyone."

"Good," said Teresa. "That's a good instinct."

"How did you know you could do what it takes?" asked Roberto. "How did you know you were that strong?"

"I didn't. But I am alive. My mother says life is a test, and today is the exam. All I can do is try my best."

"I knew someone who wanted to be a *partigiano*. My friend Maurizio. He was an army deserter. But when the Germans captured us, they shot him."

"Many of the *partigiani* were soldiers in the Fascist army once," said Teresa. "Tell me about this friend of yours. Tell me from the very beginning of the story."

Roberto talked as they walked back to the farmhouse. He told Teresa everything. She was the first person he'd told these things to, and he found he was hungry to tell them, in detail. He told every memory that had come to him when he'd worked the hill field the week before. He was grateful for an ear that might come close to understanding.

When he finished, she told him stories—about heroes of the resistance. The stories felt close and real. Ivano was one of those heroes now. The words of his letter repeated in Roberto's head. A giant beast roamed the north of Italy. Resisting the war with honor. It took so much strength to have honor.

Then Teresa sang. And the music ran through Roberto's veins like liquid iron. He joined her.

The next morning, Teresa put on her dress, freshly washed by Rina, and Roberto put on his regular farm clothes. But he also had shoes. Rina had stuffed the toes with paper, because they were too big for him. And he had a small wad of money in his pocket. Teresa had given it to him. She said money could help out when you least expected it.

No one spoke at breakfast. Everything had been said already the night before. Rina had protested for hours. It was over. Roberto couldn't be dissuaded.

They kissed good-bye to Rina and Emilio and Angelo and Manfreddo.

"This way, Lupo—'wolf'," said the girl, using Roberto's new war name for the first time, anointing him. She'd said he needed a name that would make him strong enough for whatever was ahead. A wolf was strong.

That's who he was now: Lupo. No more Roberto. And she was Volpe Rossa. No more Teresa.

Volpe Rossa pointed. "This way's north."

Lupo turned obediently.

·15·

THEY FOLLOWED THE LINES OF TREES between farmers' fields up through the valley, giving a wide berth to farmhouses and fields that were being worked. They passed rabbits and deer and, once, a startled boar, who paused and seemed to consider charging them, but then trotted away.

Pretty soon they came to a dirt road that went north. They couldn't have been walking for even an hour when they spied a cart coming toward them. Lupo grabbed Volpe Rossa's arm and tried to pull her off the road, out of sight.

"Don't be stupid," she hissed. "They might have seen us already. Act normal. And if you don't know what to say, shut up."

The cart moved maddeningly slowly. Lupo stared. It was pulled by a donkey, with a boy leading. Just a simple boy. As it passed, the boy slowed and leered at Volpe Rossa, like any teenage boy would in Venice. She lifted her chin and walked faster, like any pretty girl would in Venice. The whole thing was so normal, Lupo had to swallow to keep down a laugh of relief.

The boy jerked on the donkey's lead rope. The donkey brayed.

The sun was gently warm. Birds sang. "Are there other songs the *partigiani* sing?" asked Lupo.

"Lots. Here, let me teach you 'Bella Ciao'—beautiful goodbye. It's a good tune to march to."

They sang softly. Lupo was quick at learning the words.

A motor scooter whined behind them.

"Don't look back." Volpe Rossa skipped a few steps.

"What are you doing, skipping?"

"Shut up. You're my dumb little brother."

The whine of the scooter annoyed like a bee. Lupo felt itchy everywhere. Who was on that scooter?

The motor noise went lower in pitch as the scooter slowed down. *"Halt!"*

But Volpe Rossa didn't halt. She skipped and curled her shoulder forward, looking coyly over it at the German soldier. "*Guten Morgen*—Good morning," she said in German, rolling her *r* ridiculously, as though she was making fun of how Italians speak German.

The scooter was putting along so slow now, it coughed.

"Where are you going?" the soldier asked in Italian. The submachine gun on his back hung from a strap that went across his chest. Lupo had to force his eyes away from it.

"On a picnic." Volpe Rossa twirled around flirtatiously. "I love picnics. So does my little brother."

The soldier glanced at Lupo and back at Volpe Rossa. "He's not so little."

"Which is good," said Volpe Rossa. "That way no one bothers me."

Lupo looked at Volpe Rossa uncertainly. Was he supposed to do something to show he could defend her honor if necessary? His chest tightened.

The soldier stopped the scooter. He put one foot on the ground to steady it. Then he tapped the metal tip of his boot against the inside of the front fender. It made little clanks. "Show me your picnic."

Volpe Rossa took the string bag from Lupo, and the soldier quickly slung his gun around and pointed it at her. She opened the bag slowly and her eyes lit up. "Do you like sausage?"

"Take a bite. And your brother, too."

Volpe Rossa unwrapped a sausage and held it in two fingers, delicately. Lupo had never seen a woman eat meat with her hands before. Women didn't touch their food with their hands while they were eating. Even fruit called for a fork and knife. And a sandwich had to be held with a napkin. Only men took food with their hands, and then only when they were outside together. Or drunk. But there was Volpe Rossa, with that sausage in her fingers. It was almost obscene. She took a mincing bite and smiled at the soldier. Then she held it out to Lupo. He grabbed it with his whole hand and took a big, decisive bite.

The soldier swung the gun around to his back again. "I thought you might be a *Saujude*—a swine Jew—but you're not a pig, you eat pig. Like any good Christian." He laughed. "You're just a foolish girl and her stupid brother." He rode away.

As soon as he was out of hearing distance, Volpe Rossa said, "He's the pig." Then she pressed her lips together. "Look how smart Rina was. She gave us sausage—she knew it would protect us." And she sang.

At midday, they came across a farmhouse with a well out to the side. Lupo headed straight for it.

Volpe Rossa caught him by the elbow. "See the laundry?"

Sheets fluttered in the breeze.

"No pillowcases. See?"

"So what?" said Lupo.

"So maybe nothing. But it could be a warning. Good people hang laundry in a way that doesn't make sense, to tell *partigiani*, 'Stay away. Fascists are visiting.' We'll be careful."

Lupo closed his dry mouth and tried to get his mind off his thirst.

Soon enough they came across a stream, where they stopped and ate the sausage between slices of polenta. They drank deeply, then continued, keeping to fields as much as possible, singing softly.

In the early evening, they were on a back road when they saw a farmhouse directly ahead. "You're my older brother this time," said Volpe Rossa. "You speak. After so long at Rina's, you can talk like a local. You can sound just like them. Ask for dinner. Say as little as possible."

A farmer opened to the knocks.

"Good evening, sir," said Lupo. "My sister and I were passing and it's the dinner hour. Our hands are empty. Could you spare a piece of bread?"

Volpe Rossa had arranged her braids so they fell over her breasts. She looked young and defenseless. Her face was solemn and worried. The farmer's wife came up behind him. The two of them looked from Lupo to Volpe Rossa.

"Are you Catholic?" asked the woman. Then she put out her hand to stop him from answering. "No, no, don't say a word. It doesn't matter. Stay there. I'll get bread."

"There's room at the table," said the man, opening the door wide.

The woman stopped halfway to the table. She wrung her hands.

“Come in.” The man stepped back politely. “Please.”

Lupo went in with Volpe Rossa at his heels. The couple had clearly already finished eating, but some soup remained in a pot. And there was an end of bread.

Lupo quickly filled his mouth. He was hungry. But more than that, he wanted to have an excuse not to answer questions right away. Eating would give him a chance to think and answer smartly. Volpe Rossa was smart. Lupo was determined not to be a burden to her.

But the farm couple didn’t ask questions.

When they finished eating, Lupo and Volpe Rossa thanked the couple and went out the door. Daylight was fading fast.

Volpe Rossa looked back over her shoulder. “They’re not watching. That’s a good sign. They don’t want to know which way we’ve gone. They’re decent. Good people.”

“Maybe we should ask to sleep in their barn,” said Lupo. “See it there?” He pointed to the low wooden building.

“No. We don’t ask. Let’s just do it.”

They headed for the barn. It was surrounded by a wide swath of mud. It stank. Hogs.

“Hogs can be vicious,” said Lupo.

They walked off into a field, instead, and lay down in the open.

Lupo’s first day as a *partigiano* was over. He had food in

his stomach and nothing horrible had happened. Nothing horrible.

An owl called intermittently. A *gufo*—Ivano's war name.

Oh Lord.

Lupo put his hands over his ears and slept.

16

VOLPE ROSSA LED THEM from the dirt road to a paved one. By noon they saw a big town ahead.

An Italian policeman rode up beside them on a bicycle. "Good day," he said.

Volpe Rossa hardly looked at him. Lupo was surprised. It seemed she had a different persona for every encounter.

"Good day," Lupo finally said.

"What are you doing, going into town?"

"What everyone does in town," said Lupo.

"Then you might as well go home," said the policeman.

"And why is that?" asked Lupo.

"The shops are closed. All over Italy. It's a general strike." He sighed. "No one's got money, and the rations are too little. And now the few who have jobs aren't working, so they'll have even less money." He cycled away.

They walked steadily and stopped when they reached the edge of a large piazza. Dozens of people milled about. Some stood with arms crossed at the chest belligerently. Some carried signs saying PANE E LAVORO—bread and work. Others held signs against the rationing of basic foods.

From a road at the far corner of the piazza German police came riding through on motor scooters. They pointed guns at the demonstrators. Guns! Everyone ran.

Volpe Rossa walked quickly down an alley.

Lupo had to run to catch up. "What's going on?"

"You keep surprising me with what you don't know. Mass meetings have been forbidden for months now. The police are supposed to shoot to kill."

"Kill? For carrying signs?"

"They killed twenty-three workers in Bari and nine in Reggio." She wove in and out of small streets. At one point Lupo was sure they'd passed this way before. Then she went into a coffee bar. Lupo followed, peering hesitantly into the dark of the inside, after the bright sun. Volpe Rossa waved to the man behind the counter, who gave a little flick of the chin in welcome. She went to the back of the room and down a narrow set of stairs.

Cots lined up in the cellar. Most held men who were talking to one another in soft voices. Bandaged men. This was a makeshift clinic. The men looked up with silent fear on their faces. Two women stood by a food table and stared, too. It wasn't Volpe Rossa who scared all of them; they looked right past her to Lupo.

Just that pause in the conversation brought a tall woman rushing in from a side room. She stopped when she saw Lupo. Her eyes passed to Volpe Rossa. She wiped her hands on her apron and leaned against the wall, as though she might collapse without its support.

"It's okay," said Volpe Rossa. "Lupo's with me."

The women at the table turned now and continued their work. One ladled pasta into bowls; the other covered them with beans and tomatoes. Volpe Rossa went and kissed them on each cheek. Then she kissed the woman leaning against the wall. She went from man to man, kissing hello. And she served the bowls to the men. They fell to talking again and ate.

Lupo still stood at the foot of the stairs. The smell of the food made his tongue feel thick. He and Volpe Rossa hadn't eaten yet today.

After Volpe Rossa served the last man, she brought a bowl to Lupo. He sat on the floor and shoveled the delicious food into his mouth.

"If there are ever Germans watching, eat standing up," said Volpe Rossa. "Jews never stand when they eat." She got a bowl and perched on the edge of a bed to eat. The other women did the same.

When he'd finished, Lupo helped carry the pots into a small kitchen. The three women washed up, moving around one another with intimacy, as though they'd been friends all their lives.

Their talk turned to the real business fast. There were two possible jobs Volpe Rossa and Lupo could help do. One would carry them northwest to Rome. The other would carry them northeast, much farther, all the way to Florence. The second was more perilous—but, then, nothing was without danger.

"We'll go to Florence," said Volpe Rossa.

Florence was closer to Venice. Lupo wondered if Volpe Rossa had made the choice for his sake.

The next morning Lupo found himself on a bicycle, pulling a milk cart behind. He had hated waiting to start the journey. It was better to act fast on decisions that scared him. But no one would deliver milk at any time other than morning. So there was no choice.

Volpe Rossa was on a bicycle, too, but she rode ahead of him, and she didn't pull a cart. Her bicycle had a wire basket with another basket inside it—a large woven one.

Lupo's cart held five rifles, under a layer of straw, with milk jugs on top and an oilcloth covering it all. Volpe Rossa's basket held sticks of dynamite under a pile of ribbons. Her hair was tied in ribbons, too. They were to deliver everything to a farmhouse halfway to the next town. And they had a rule, the only rule of the *partigiani*: do your job. There was no discussion of at what price. They were to deliver their cargo. Period.

The irony of Lupo, who hated guns, carrying these rifles didn't escape him. But guns could be used to stop violence as well as to do violence. That's what Volpe Rossa said. That's what Lupo held on to.

A kilometer before the farmhouse they'd see a pile of stones beside the road. That's how they'd recognize it.

They had been on the road only half an hour when they heard a car behind them.

Lupo pedaled hard and came up beside Volpe Rossa. He hooted at her lasciviously. That was their game.

If the car held Germans, Volpe Rossa was supposed to answer in Italian—because Germans couldn't tell one Italian dialect from another. But if the car held Italians, then Lupo had to be the one to answer.

The car pulled alongside them. "Young lady," called the German officer in Italian. "Is he bothering you?"

"I'm managing." Volpe Rossa gave the officer a smile.

"Get out of the way, boy," said the officer. "I want to speak to this young woman. Can't you see that?"

Lupo fell back a little.

"A girl as pretty as you is target practice for these bumpkins," shouted the officer over the rumble of the car motor. "How about I throw your bicycle in my trunk and give you a lift wherever you're going?"

"You're generous," said Volpe Rossa. "But you have important things to do. And I can handle boys like him."

The officer pulled his car in front of Volpe Rossa's bicycle and stopped, blocking her way. He got out.

Volpe Rossa put her hand behind the small of her back and secretly waved Lupo on, past her.

Lupo pedaled around them. His ears rang with fear. He dared to look back. Volpe Rossa held her basket and the officer was putting her bicycle in his car trunk.

No!

Should Lupo stop?

He looked back again. The officer's hand was on Volpe Rossa's back as she stepped up into the car. His hand slid down her body.

Lupo looked straight ahead and pedaled faster.

The rule was do your job. That was the only rule. And his job was to deliver those guns. If he did something rash, both he and Volpe Rossa would be in trouble for sure.

Right now she might be in trouble and she might not.

No. He knew she was in trouble. That officer's hand told him.

The German's car zoomed past, up the road.

Tears blurred Lupo's vision. Volpe Rossa had to know how to take care of herself. She had to.

He pedaled and pedaled.

Volpe Rossa was in a German officer's car.

He pedaled and pedaled.

He was alone.

Again.

He'd been alone so many times, and still the sense of desperation never lessened. If another German officer came, he had no game to play now—no Volpe Rossa to pretend to be flirting with.

He wiped away his tears and pedaled furiously. He passed clusters of houses, and wagons now and then. Men on scooters whizzed by. And one car.

He'd been pedaling for hours, searching the sides of the road. Had he missed the pile of stones? What if someone had moved them? A sour taste filled his mouth. He was sure he'd missed it now. Stupid stupid stupid him. He couldn't do it without Volpe Rossa.

And there it was. Finally. Such a little pile. Only a kilometer more. He pedaled right up to the farmhouse.

The farmer's wife was outside before he got off the bicycle. She was enormously pregnant. She put her hands on either side of her belly and looked up and down the road. "Bring it into the barn."

· 17 ·

LUPO LAY ON OLD STRAW in the barn. He couldn't fall asleep. Fear swirled in his head. Volpe Rossa was gone. He had failed her. He knew that now. The rule might be to do your job, but how could anyone do their job if their partners abandoned them? He should have done something.

The wide wagon beside him held a layer of rifles under a false bottom—guns that had accumulated there from milk carts over the past few weeks.

He'd be given another job in the morning. A job involving all those rifles.

That was crazy. Lupo had no experience at this *partigiano* thing. He was lousy at it. He needed Volpe Rossa. Without her, he was a bumbler. No good to anyone.

If she didn't show up, he'd get back on the road to Venice. Head home. He had never stopped wanting to do that the whole time he was at Rina's—he had just planned to wait till the Germans were gone first. But at the rate this war was going, they might never be gone.

He rolled onto one side. Then onto the other side. Then onto his back again.

Samuele had died. Maurizio had died. Ivano had died. Anytime Lupo loved someone, they died. He'd be better off never caring about anyone. And if Volpe Rossa was still alive, she was better off without him.

It was true. He couldn't save anyone. So there was no point trying. And there was no reason he should feel so ashamed of his thoughts right now.

He stared unblinking until his eyes burned. He needed to sleep. He was too tired to think straight.

The barn back at Rina's farm had been a good place to sleep. This barn would be good, too, if he only let it. He opened his senses to the barn.

Horses weren't as noisy as oxen, but they swished their tails and stamped. And one of these four horses had the habit of throwing back its head and snorting.

The barn door creaked loudly. Lupo lay dead still.

"Lupo?" came Volpe Rossa's whisper.

He ran to her and they clung together in the dark. She was here. Breathing warm and strong. Lupo went weak with relief. "How did you get away?"

"He let me off in the next town. But I had to wait till I was sure he was long gone. Then I pedaled back."

"Let's go up to the farmhouse. You must be hungry."

"He fed me." She pulled away. Then she walked past him and lay down on the straw.

Lupo lay beside her. "Did he . . . Are you all right?"

"I'm always all right."

"No one's always all right."

"I am."

"I shouldn't have left you. I'm sorry."

Volpe Rossa sat up. "Don't talk stupid. You did your job. And we're both still alive."

"I'm glad you're alive. I was so afraid."

"Don't waste your energies worrying about me. Ever." She lay back down.

"What happened to the basket with the dynamite?"

"I found a good person in town. I gave it to her. Riding back with it would have been too risky. He might have passed me again." Her voice broke. She rolled onto her side, so her back was to Lupo. "So I didn't do my job. But you did yours. And these are good people. Sleep now." Her voice sounded defeated.

Lupo wanted to touch her shoulder, to comfort her. But he didn't dare.

After a while, he sang in a hush. Volpe Rossa joined him.

When they finished, they lay there in silence.

"Lupo," whispered Volpe Rossa after a long while, "I'm glad you're alive, too."

* * *

In the morning, the pregnant woman climbed onto the wagon bench with Volpe Rossa by her side. She never told them her name. Lupo sat in the wagon with two bicycles. If they were stopped, the story was that they were delivering the wagon to a farmer outside the next town—whatever the next town might be at that point—and the bicycles were so that the woman and girl could return home, while the boy stayed to help the farmer.

They left the woman's two brothers behind, only twelve and fourteen years old. They would take care of the farm chores in her absence. They'd even return the milk cart Lupo had brought. Nobody fretted over leaving everything in the hands of mere boys; it was clear this had happened before.

All day long German jeeps and cars passed in greater numbers the farther north they went. The cars slowed down, but when the Germans saw that big pregnant belly, they tipped their military hats and went on.

The woman had told Lupo that pregnancy put a woman beyond suspicion, but he hadn't really believed it—not till now. He knew enough of war to suspect anyone and everyone. Why didn't those German soldiers know the same?

The wagon made slow progress, though they didn't stop except once, to eat. The roads wound through hills, past small towns. Trees bloomed white and pink and purple everywhere. Grasslands waved red with poppies. Lupo's arms and legs flexed. So much pent-up energy. He wanted to be back on Rina's farm, hoeing, planting, working himself into physical exhaustion. Riding in this pokey wagon made him feel half-mad.

That night Volpe Rossa and Lupo slept in another barn, fed by more good people, as Volpe Rossa called them. The pregnant woman slept in this new farmhouse, with the family. At dawn, she got on a bicycle to ride back. It wasn't one from the wagon—no, those had to stay put, as props for their act if Germans stopped them. This bicycle was extra, for general use. It was a good system; someone rode a bike in one direction, and then left it; someone else soon came along and rode it back in the other direction.

The pregnant woman said she'd get home by afternoon. Lupo watched till she rounded a curve, out of sight.

The new farm woman turned to Lupo with a circumspect smile. "You haven't developed a stomach for this yet, eh? Don't worry. She's far enough along that if she needs help, anyone will give it. And she's not so far along that an upset will cause a premature delivery. We're careful that way. We've learned the limits."

They'd learned. Oh, Lord, the price of lessons.

The next day started as a repeat of the last, only this

woman wasn't pregnant. She was remarkably pretty, though. And she unbraided Volpe Rossa's hair and brushed it shiny and fluffy and dressed her in clean clothes.

They hadn't been on the road an hour when a pair of Nazi officers stopped them. The Germans spoke good Italian, and the Italian girls flirted outrageously. They could both have careers in cinema after the war, Lupo was sure.

One of the Germans asked Volpe Rossa, "What do you want most, a girl like you?"

Volpe Rossa put prayer hands together at her chin, as though in thought. "A piece of cake. And, oh, yes"—she curled a shoulder forward coquettishly, like Lupo had watched her do before—"with whipped cream."

The officers laughed and talked in German about how foolish Italians were. They gave the girls German sausages and stale pastries, then left with a lustful backward leer.

When they were out of hearing distance, the farm woman laughed. "*Che schifo*—what disgusting stuff," she said as she scooped the soldiers' food together.

"We could get hungry later," said Lupo.

"Don't worry. I don't throw anything away."

"You never know what could be useful," added Volpe Rossa.

Later her words proved true. A German soldier, alone on a scooter, pulled them over and interrogated them without showing the least susceptibility to the girls' charms. He was large and maybe forty years old. Stern and businesslike. He spoke only German, so Lupo had to be the one to deal with him.

"We're delivering this wagon to a farmer," said Lupo, in broken German. After all, how would a farm boy have learned good German?

The soldier came around the back of the wagon. "Empty?" He jiggled a side hard. "Nothing hidden under here?" He brushed straw away and exposed a swath of the bottom—the false bottom.

Volpe Rossa unwrapped the German food from that morning. "Here, here, brother," she said to Lupo in Italian, twisting and passing him the food. "Please offer this fine man the food our friends prepared for us."

Lupo held the food out to the soldier. "Would you like something to eat?"

The soldier looked dubious. "German officers' food? How did you get it?"

"Friends of my sisters—they gave it to us. You're welcome to as much as you want."

The soldier stuck a whole pastry in his mouth. He wiped the sugar from his lips with the back of his hand. "Everything looks in order here." He got on his scooter and drove away.

And so it went, day after day, always with a new woman on the bench beside Volpe Rossa—a woman who spoke the local dialect and returned home the next morning. It took five full days to deliver the rifles to Florence. But they did it. With the help of good people.

18

VOLPE ROSSA AND LUPO STOOD near the front of the noisy crowd outside Fascist headquarters, which was directly across the piazza from the hotel the Nazis had taken over for their headquarters. An empty net shopping bag hung from Volpe Rossa's wrist. A larger sack was slung over Lupo's shoulder.

They were with the middle-aged, matronly woman who had taken them in the night before, when they'd finally arrived in Florence. She introduced herself as Giovanni's mother—that's all. Lupo was accustomed to that by now. Many of the resistance women he'd met identified themselves as someone's mother, wife, sister. Giovanni's mother. Probably something awful had happened to Giovanni.

Giovanni's mother made a tsking noise and pointed with her chin. Lupo and Volpe Rossa looked. A woman of maybe twenty-five crossed the piazza in a fancy dress. Her legs were shiny. She hurried into the Nazi headquarters.

"Silk stockings," said Volpe Rossa. Her lip curled in disgust.

"What's so bad about stockings?" asked Lupo.

"She's not hungry, that's what. Where do you think she gets them? What do you think she's going to do in that Nazi hotel?"

"She's the enemy," mumbled Giovanni's mother. Then she let out a tired sigh. "This system makes no sense. We wait hours to get coupons from the Fascists, only so we can change lines and wait hours to buy milk, fuel, supplies."

"If we're lucky," said the young woman in front of them. She was pregnant. Two small children clung to her skirts. "The last two times I came, when I got up to the front, the official announced there were no more coupons. They'd run out. Can you imagine?" She held up her shopping basket. "I went home with this basket empty. That's why I came early today. I was here before the sun."

"The whole system stinks," said Giovanni's mother.

Lupo and Volpe Rossa exchanged glances. That was dangerous talk. You never knew who might overhear. Volpe Rossa put her hand on Giovanni's mother's arm.

Giovanni's mother brushed it off in quick annoyance. "Don't you have anyone you can leave the children with, so at least they don't have to spend all this time waiting?"

The pregnant woman shook her head. "My husband's at home—out of work, like everyone else. But he's sick in bed.

My brother is off somewhere in Germany, slaving for those Nazis. My other brother's in prison in Russia—if he's still alive. And . . . well, why should I tell you? You know how it is. We all know. Everyone's miserable." She reached into her basket and came out with a handful of boiled chestnuts. The children immediately set to peeling and eating them.

The crowd suddenly hushed. A Nazi officer had come up. He worked his way through the people, asking to see documents. Everyone fumbled with purses and dug around in bags.

Lupo's mouth twitched involuntarily. He had phony documents. So did Volpe Rossa. So far he'd avoided having to show them. Were they up to snuff? He'd seen people dragged away because their documents weren't in order.

Volpe Rossa touched the back of Giovanni's mother's hand. Their eyes met.

When the officer got to the front of the crowd, Giovanni's mother took the documents from Volpe Rossa and Lupo and added them under hers. She handed all three to the officer at once and put a hand on her forehead, as though she had a splitting headache. "When is this door going to open, officer?" Her voice was a shrill whine.

"Yes, when?" chimed in Volpe Rossa. "We've been waiting hours. Can't you teach these Italian Fascists some of your German efficiency?"

The officer shrugged and gave a little laugh. He checked

the top document and handed all three back to Giovanni's mother without opening the other two. He glanced at the documents of the pregnant woman and left.

The crowd went back to talking among themselves, but quietly now.

Finally the door of the Fascist headquarters opened. But not wide enough for everyone to rush in and press together in front of the coupon table. Instead, an officer stepped outside and closed the door behind him. He stood straight in his black shirt and beret with a skull on the front, and bellowed, "Go home, everyone. The coupons aren't ready yet."

Angry mutterings came from all sides.

"Go home," said the officer. He waved them away. "Get out of here. Come back later."

"No!" The pregnant woman pulled a rolling pin out of her shopping basket and held it over her head.

Lupo's face went slack. She was pregnant with two children to protect. Had she lost her mind?

The woman shook the rolling pin. "I will not go away empty-handed again. I came prepared."

A rolling pin? The Fascist officer had a gun in the holster at his waist and a rifle slung across his back. Who did she think could help her? The crowd watched, alert, tense—but they were unarmed.

But the pregnant woman didn't seem to be looking for help. She swung that rolling pin high, wielding it like a bat, as though she thought she was a real threat. "Mussolini is supposed to protect the family. He told women to stay home and have children. That's what the Fascists have been saying for two decades. Well, look at me. Look at my children." Her voice rose to a shout. "I'm not leaving without coupons."

The Italian officer put his hand on the hilt of his gun.

Lupo felt Volpe Rossa stiffen beside him. He took her arm to still her, but he already knew it was useless.

"She's right," said Volpe Rossa loudly.

That was it. Volpe Rossa would get arrested now, too. Well, he'd failed her before. He'd never do it again. "We need coupons," said Lupo in a croak. For a moment he couldn't hear anything but a buzz inside his head.

Then, "We all have families," came the call from the back of the crowd. "Look at us."

"Coupons," said another voice.

"Coupons," joined more voices, louder. "Coupons, coupons."

The crowd chanted now. "Coupons, coupons, coupons."

The pregnant woman still brandished that rolling pin.

The officer looked stunned. "All right," he said at last. "I'll open the door, and those who are here right now have to rush in so I can close the door fast. We have enough coupons for you, but not for anyone else." He opened the door, and the crowd pushed through.

Later, as they were leaving, Volpe Rossa came up on one

side of the pregnant woman and Giovanni's mother came up on the other. Lupo followed. They walked her and the children to the milk store.

"You've got courage," said Volpe Rossa.

"And the right reaction to desperation," said Giovanni's mother. "Join us."

The woman stopped. She looked at her children. Then she shook her head. "It's true, I can't stand this anymore." She laughed. "And what else have I got to do?"

And so the resistance grew. One ordinary, desperate person at a time.

· 19 ·

LUPO AND VOLPE ROSSA changed homes often, to protect their hosts. Florence offered lots of hosts.

They spent weeks secretly dispersing those rifles around town. Lupo delivered some in shopping bags with lettuce on top. Volpe Rossa delivered some wrapped in blankets in baby carriages.

Not batting an eye, they walked past German soldiers and tanks. Lupo didn't know how Volpe Rossa got up the nerve to do it. He always had to fight the urge to run, to run and run, all the way to Venice. What kept him here was the power of song; he recited *partigiano* songs in his head. But it wasn't the words that mattered now—it was simply their very existence. Songs filled his head and pushed aside everything else.

Lupo hadn't seen those rifles in action, but he heard the news of what they did. A German jeep outside town had been shot at from who knew where. A truck had had its tires blown out. A group of drunken Nazi soldiers had been ambushed in the night. *Partigiano* rifles were nothing in an open showdown against German submachine guns. But these weren't open showdowns. These were snipings—the only kind of warfare possible when the scales were so unbalanced.

Lupo lay in bed late one morning, thinking about that imbalance. He knew it was a mistake to dwell on it; it would only disable him, keep him pinned to that bed.

He got up, and his gaze happened to go out the window. Nazi soldiers marched Italian men down the street. Lupo didn't recognize anyone, of course, but he knew what was going on. The Italian men were surely known anti-Fascists. The Nazis were marching them to the train station, to put them on cattle cars that would carry them to prisons in Mantova and Belluno. These processions happened often. This was the second one down this street since he'd been at this host's home—and he'd been here only five days.

One of the men was wounded and stumbled along. As they passed under Lupo's window, he fell. Clearly, he couldn't walk another step. A Nazi shot him.

A spasm went through Lupo's shoulders.

From a window on the other side of the road, someone shot the Nazi. Lupo saw the rifle disappear back inside.

The other Nazi soldiers quickly gunned out the windows on that side of the street—all the windows, even though they, too, surely saw that rifle, so they knew which window the shot had come from. The air shook. A high-pitched wail circled everything. The officer in charge motioned them ahead, and the procession continued on to the station.

"We must do something," whispered Volpe Rossa. Lupo hadn't even realized she'd been standing there. She squeezed his arm.

And he knew she was right.

At mealtime that evening, Volpe Rossa walked into Nazi headquarters. She just walked right in, through the front door, an apron tied around her waist. She was going to find the list of anti-Fascists and change the names on it—make up phony names—so people couldn't be rounded up and marched off to prison.

Lupo waited for her in the piazza. His breath was raspy with fear. He had no instructions. He had no weapon on him—only his phony documents and a small wad of money. If she got into a jam, he would do whatever he could. He'd think fast, because he had to think fast. Please, let him be able to think fast.

Neither of them had been in these Nazi headquarters before. But hotels had a lot in common. And Lupo had described to Volpe Rossa how the Nazi headquarters at the

hotel in Naples had been arranged. The office would surely be on the ground floor behind the reception desk in plain view of anyone coming out of the dining room. The kitchen would be on the far side of that dining room. So a kitchen helper, as Volpe Rossa was pretending to be, would have no excuse for being near the front office. But if she acted like she knew what she was doing, like she had a right to be there, maybe. . . . That was her plan, at least.

The piazza was empty, of course. Everyone was home eating. The quality of the air slowly changed. Lupo could feel early evening on his arms and cheeks. Volpe Rossa was taking too long.

He wanted to run. But for the first time since he'd joined the resistance, his impulse was to dash toward danger, not away. To race in there and grab her, protect her. His lips pressed shut hard to hold in a shout.

And there she was, coming out the front door, walking lightly, seemingly not even in a hurry.

Lupo started toward her.

A Nazi officer came out the door after her. He drew his gun. *"Halt!"*

She stopped, slowly turned, and tilted her head at him.

He kept the gun pointed at her—that mesmerizing gun—and he spoke. In German. Lupo could hear, because there was no other noise in the piazza. The officer was asking what

she had been doing. He'd seen her coming out of the office, hadn't he? What was she doing there?

Lupo pulled his focus away from the gun. He dug the money out of his pocket and curled it in his fist. He ran up to them. "Were you with that officer again, sister?" he said angrily in Italian to Volpe Rossa. "Papà will be so mad. Mamma will cry."

"No!" Volpe Rossa shook her head frantically. "I was helping in the kitchen. See my apron."

"You're lying." Lupo grabbed Volpe Rossa roughly by the arm and reached his other hand down the front of her bodice, then pulled out his hand and opened his fist. The paper money swelled like a blooming flower. He slapped her across the face.

The officer holstered his gun. He shook his head and took the money. "If she wants a career at this," he said in German to Lupo, "tell your sister to use her next pay on a pretty dress. Even I would be interested in her if she cleaned up a bit. In fact, I'll be on the lookout for her." He pinched Volpe Rossa on the cheek that was still red from where Lupo had slapped her, and went back into headquarters.

"We can't stay in Florence," said Lupo, hurrying Volpe Rossa through the streets toward home. "It's too dangerous now."

"But there's so much work to be done in this city," said

Volpe Rossa. “For the past few months we’ve been running constantly. They need us.”

“No. You won’t walk past those Nazi headquarters again. Ever.”

“You’re worrying about me. I told you. You can’t afford to—”

“No!”

20

THE NEXT DAY LUPO AND VOLPE ROSSA drove a wagon full of munitions from a farmhouse outside Florence to another on the edge of the city of Bologna.

Immediately they took on the job of delivering the wagon cargo to members of the resistance scattered around the city. Lupo dug out the inside of loaves of bread, stuffed them with dynamite, and turned them upside down into bags, so that the unbroken end of the loaf showed. He carried the bags in broad daylight.

Volpe Rossa put a dozen pistols in a cloth sling over her shoulder and walked it straight across a busy piazza, smiling at the Nazi soldiers she passed, as brazen as could be. Anyone who saw her and thought for just a moment could tell that sling held something heavy, something suspect. But the soldiers never seemed to think when they looked at Volpe Rossa. All they saw was a beautiful girl.

But even though only one at a time delivered the munitions each day, they worked as a team; the other one was always nearby, ready to swoop if trouble came.

Once when Lupo was carrying a sack of dynamite-stuffed bread, a Nazi soldier stopped him and tapped the end of a loaf. He put his hand around it to pull it out of the bag.

But Volpe Rossa called to the soldier from nearby, "Hey." She waved, wiggling her fingers in the air. "Big boy," she said in lilting Italian. "Hungry?" She carried her own sack of real baked goods. "Wouldn't you prefer a coconut tart?" And she offered one, blushing and blinking.

Lupo never understood how she could bring color to her cheeks so quickly. The Nazi fell for it. And Lupo couldn't understand that, either. How could it be that time after time Germans assumed Italian women were mindless?

Everywhere Lupo went he kept his ears open for information about the *partigiani* activities. Underground radio programs came from the mountains of Tuscany.

He kept his eyes open, too. Underground newspapers came from Milan.

Then Bologna started its own paper. Sometimes Lupo helped deliver it, so he met the people who worked on it. Women, all women. They told Lupo women were putting out underground papers all over Italy. He wondered if his mother was working on a paper in Venice. She used to march in war protests; she'd have the courage to write for an underground paper.

Lupo read about how the *partigiani* blew up viaducts and bridges and railroads. They sneaked Jews north into Switzerland, walking over mountains. They stopped trains full of prisoners because of "mechanical problems"—but really they stopped them to help prisoners escape. They ambushed supply vehicles.

He read how in Verona and Padua, towns near Venice, people made posters about the need for a new constitution. With democratic elections. At night people plastered those posters on town walls, and the next day the Nazis ripped them down. But they reappeared by morning.

Knowing these things helped Lupo. His tasks were small, but they were part of something giant. The giant beast of the resistance that sang in his head at night. What he did mattered. It mattered politically, for Italy. But it also mattered personally, for the memory of Ivano and Maurizio and, especially, Samuele. His best friend. His Jewish friend, who had died in Ukraine. He thought about Samuele a lot. All it took was the sight of a Jewish armband to trigger those memories.

There was but a handful of Jews left in Bologna. But the handful dared to walk outside. They were forced to wear armbands with a yellow star. Samuele had an armband like that. He had taken it off before they were kidnapped.

Lupo had been in Bologna three weeks already when he sat down on a park bench to wait for Volpe Rossa. An old man with an armband came up carrying a chair. The man set the chair by the end of the bench and dropped onto it with a tired "ooof."

"What?" said Lupo, spreading his hands half in question, half in offering. "I'm not so fat that we can't both sit on the bench side by side."

The old man waved Lupo's remark off, but his face stayed agreeable. "I've come to this bench every day for seventeen years. Now they tell me Jews aren't allowed to sit on a public bench. So I bring my chair."

"That's absurd."

The old man looked at Lupo with bleary eyes. "They call us *Untermenschen*. It means 'subhumans.'"

Volpe Rossa came rushing up.

Lupo stood. "Meet my friend," he said to Volpe Rossa.

"Excuse my not getting up," said the old man.

They shook hands. No one exchanged names.

Volpe Rossa bit her bottom lip and glanced around. "Do you have family here?"

"Not any longer."

She looked at Lupo meaningfully. But Lupo didn't understand what could be on her mind. The *partigiani* could never help this man escape to Switzerland. He was too old to travel like that.

"If you want to take off that armband, we'll hide you," she whispered, though no one was near enough to hear.

"And live in a cupboard?" The old man waved off her words, like he'd waved off Lupo's. "I used to publish books—very fine books—but they won't let me anymore. I wear an armband. I'm not allowed at public events. And when I die, the newspapers will not be allowed to announce my death. But right now I'm alive. I walk around. I hear the birds. I breathe the fresh air."

Volpe Rossa pursed her lips. "If—"

The old man took her wrist. "Hush. Help the young Jews, if you can find any. They're the future." He let go and folded his hands in his lap. "Go on now. Don't get caught talking to me."

Volpe Rossa stood there.

Finally Lupo dragged her away.

· 21 ·

WEEKS SOMEHOW BECAME MONTHS. April 25 came and went, and Lupo turned fifteen without a whisper. Spring ended; hot weather came. Through it all, Lupo and Volpe Rossa worked faithfully. They reported daily to Dario's sister, the *partigiana* woman in charge of this part of town.

One morning Dario's sister looked at Lupo in dismay. "Every day you grow taller."

Lupo shrugged. Yes, he was bigger. He no longer had paper stuffed in the tips of the boots Rina had given him.

Dario's sister shook her head. "We can't use you anymore."

"What?" Lupo reeled in shock.

"You don't look like a harmless kid anymore. You can't go out on these missions. Volpe Rossa will go alone."

"But—"

"It's too dangerous." Volpe Rossa took Lupo by the upper arms. "You're a man now."

Lupo blinked in frustration. They were right. He was suspect. The Germans stopped him on the street more and more often to look at his phony documents, which were somehow always accepted. So far, at least. But how long could that last? He was putting them all at risk.

"You can join a group in the hills," said Dario's sister. "I'll arrange it."

The *partigiani* in the hills sniped at German jeeps. Lupo would have to carry a rifle. He looked at Volpe Rossa.

Volpe Rossa turned to Dario's sister. "Not yet. He can help out here indoors."

"There's nothing for a man to do indoors," said Dario's sister.

"Then he'll do what women do. Help me, Lupo." Volpe Rossa pointed to her bicycle. "Help me load it up."

So Lupo took off the bicycle seat and tucked messages into the shaft and remounted it while Volpe Rossa tucked other messages inside her clothes. They had both delivered these kinds of messages so many times. Information about where Nazi troops were gathering, who had which equipment, what acts of sabotage the *partigiani* were planning, where and when the *partigiani* could expect a delivery of munitions from the Allies. They'd carried these past Nazi checkpoints, laughing together in relief after each time.

A painful uneasiness brought cold sweat to Lupo's cheeks and forehead. Volpe Rossa would be alone today. And from now on. If anything went wrong, he wouldn't be there to back her up.

Volpe Rossa touched a finger to his cheek. "Don't be so upset. Make yourself useful inside. And I'll tell you all about it tonight."

Her hair hung loose, forming a black cloud around her face and making her look more stunning than ever. In that moment Lupo understood why the Nazis couldn't see beyond that beauty. She took his breath away.

Then she was gone.

He threw himself into indoor work with a maniacal passion that day. He made phone calls, passing messages that way—messages about women, always women; female pseudonyms fooled the Nazi phone censors. He packed bullets for delivery, marking the paper so it was easy to match them to the right guns. He worked without pause.

Then it was evening, and Volpe Rossa was finally home again, and he breathed free, as she kept her promise and told about each task of the day.

She'd done the same thing she'd been doing all along. She passed messages to other women, meeting them in bathrooms of coffee bars. And those women rode off on their bicycles, their hair flying behind them in curls, just like Volpe Rossa's, and passed the messages to still other women. News traveled all across the north of Italy from the hand of one *staffetta*—"runner"—to the next.

Volpe Rossa had done fine. She hadn't needed Lupo.

The next day started with the same cold sweat. And the day after that, and the day after that. Lupo worked like a whirling dervish while Volpe Rossa was off on her bicycle. His job concerned bicycles, too; he repaired them for the *staffette*. And he scrubbed the old bedsheets everyone dropped off, then ripped them into bandages of various sizes for the clinics. And he helped organize burials.

At night, before going to sleep, Volpe Rossa told him of the successes and frustrations of the day. And, after a while, she told him of the near disasters, too. And that cold sweat broke out again.

He had to keep himself from worrying about her all day, or he'd lose his mind. So Lupo took on an additional task: he read underground newspapers to the men in the clinics who were too wounded to read for themselves.

He read about the Allies liberating Rome. The invasion of Normandy, in France. The return of the king to his rightful home in Rome. Life was changing at last.

The wounded in the clinics congratulated one another. The war would be over soon.

He read about the *partigiani* victories in the hills. And a massive prison break in Belluno—seventy-three political prisoners freed. Another prison break in Alba followed just days later. Groups of *partigiani* in the hills passed the news by signaling with their *falò*—small bonfires.

Everything was changing fast.

He read about the Allies liberating Orbetello and Orvieto. Then Perugia and Siena and town after town, moving north constantly. It wouldn't be long now—all Italy would be free.

Then in late July, Hitler was wounded in a failed assassination attempt. Furious, he ordered all anti-Fascists in Italy to be killed—not imprisoned—simply killed. Shot on sight.

And the news that Lupo read to the men in the clinics changed drastically.

Over the following days, five thousand *partigiani* and their sympathizers were killed. Five thousand.

In Milan and Turin, Nazis came into homes at three in the morning and shot people in their beds. Small villages that were known to be the homes of *partigiani* were burned to the ground. Corpses of *partigiani* were hung from trees and lampposts to intimidate others. And sometimes people who had nothing to do with the resistance at all were shot. Gratuitous killing. It was as though killing had become a habit. Or a disease.

Lupo read about how one of the past duties of the *partigiani* had now become a massive undertaking: letting the family of a *partigiano* know of his death and bringing them some little thing of his. And his voice cracked in sorrow. It had been only a week since the assassination attempt on Hitler, but it felt like the chaos was never ending. Each new bit of news beat him up. And it beat up all these wounded men.

In silence, he folded the newspaper and set it on a table and went up the stairs from the basement clinic into the bakery above it to get fresh air.

Through the open doorway he saw Volpe Rossa. She was coming his way slowly. On foot.

As she stepped through the doorway, he said, "Your bicycle?"

"They confiscated it at a checkpoint."

So it had finally happened; the Nazis had stopped her. Lupo held out his arms.

But Volpe Rossa didn't move into them. She seemed to sway on her feet, as though in a daze. "They searched me." Her voice was small, like the whir of a hummingbird wing. He had to strain to hear. "But it's okay," she murmured, "I had already delivered everything."

"They suspect you now, though. They must."

"So I'll work with you indoors."

"Yes," said Lupo. He walked to her and took her hands. "We'll be a team again."

They worked side by side on all those same chores but one: Lupo ceded to Volpe Rossa reading aloud the newspapers to the men in the clinics. He couldn't bear it anymore.

The news reported battles. An enormous one on the upper Secchia River became legendary overnight. The Germans had tanks, mortars, flame throwers, every sort of artillery. The *partigiani* had only one-shot rifles and a few grenades. But they had determination and they knew the terrain. In four days of fighting, fourteen hundred Nazis died, and only two hundred and fifty *partigiani* died.

Volpe Rossa read of the Allies liberating Florence. In every newspaper the slogan was bold: "*Questa è la nostra ora*—This is our hour." The men in the clinics cheered quietly. And Lupo cheered with them. He'd worked in Florence; it was partly his city. Next, the Allies liberated Pisa and many other towns of Tuscany.

Maybe it was better that Volpe Rossa was the one to read the news. Maybe she was somehow charmed, and so long as she was reading, the news would be good. Maybe if Volpe Rossa kept reading, tomorrow the Allies would liberate Bologna. And next week they'd liberate Venice. Lupo was desperate to believe that.

But then the news changed.

The Allies stopped. Though they were in Florence, they didn't come north to Bologna. Though they were in Southern France, they didn't come south into Liguria. They didn't come from any direction. They said the rains were torrential, the winds were gale force, it was impossible.

But the underground newspapers gave a different explanation. They said the Allies had set up bases in central and southern Italy from which they could attack Germany and the Balkans easily. So they didn't need the north of Italy.

And, worse, the papers said the Allies didn't want peace in the north. If the *partigiani* kept fighting the Germans in Italy, German forces would be diverted from the other war fronts—from France and Russia—and the Allies could win there.

The *partigiani* were all on their own for who knew how much longer. And everything horrible happened. The Allies bombed the northern Italian cities, trying to kill Nazis. And the Nazis bombed the northern Italian hills and mountains, raking for groups of *partigiani*.

Every semblance of sanity was gone.

22

LUPO WAS WALKING TO FASCIST HEADQUARTERS in the hopes of picking up food coupons when he saw a big cart pulled by oxen stopped in the piazza. Two priests stood arguing with the police. Lupo could hear bits and pieces. The cart had apparently been there for hours—and the police wouldn't let the priests unload it.

From under the oilcloth that covered the mound in the cart stuck a foot. The cart was full of bodies.

Lupo moved closer, till he could catch all the words. The police said the bodies should be dumped outside town and burned like garbage; they were *partigiani* bodies, after all.

Lupo's head went hot. It felt huge and hot and bursting. He walked up to the cart and pulled on the oilcloth till it covered the foot. Then he turned and continued his walk toward the Fascist headquarters.

A policeman yelled after him, "Stop!"

But Lupo felt suddenly drunk with recklessness. He kept walking.

One of the priests said loudly, "Don't bother the boy. It was an act of Catholic charity. Mussolini's still Catholic, you know. Or are you saying that that Protestant German Rudolf Rahn rules Italy rather than our own Mussolini?"

They argued.

Lupo ran.

The doors of the Fascist headquarters were still closed, and it was almost mealtime. Lupo easily lost himself in the frustrated crowd waiting for coupons.

A pair of Nazis came up to check documents. Lupo didn't flinch. His mind was still on the foot of the man in the wagon, on those bodies that might get burned like filth.

But then he saw the old man in the crowd. The Jew he'd met in the park months before. Lupo was sure it was him. And he wasn't wearing his armband. Of course not. After the assassination attempt on Hitler, the few remaining Jews in town were put on trains north. If these two Nazis looked at the old man's documents, they'd find out he was a Jew. They'd find out he'd broken the law by not wearing his armband. He was a dead man.

The Nazis moved through the crowd, telling the people they'd already checked to stay on one side. They were still a good distance from the old man.

Lupo pressed his way toward a Nazi. He showed his documents. Then he walked over to the side with the people who had already been checked. He looked around and met eyes with a woman he didn't know. Then he walked back to the side with the people who hadn't yet shown their documents. He looked over his shoulder. The woman was watching him. He showed his documents to the other Nazi. Then he walked back to the other side.

He looked around and met the eyes of two other women and a man. Then he walked back to the side with the people who hadn't yet shown their documents. And one of the women followed him. She showed her documents for a second time. And now another woman did it. Now more people milled around, from one side to the other. Pinpricks of gratitude ran up Lupo's arms.

In the glorious confusion, Lupo took the old man by the elbow and walked him to the side with the people whose documents had been checked. The old man didn't question what Lupo was doing. He stood beside Lupo docilely, as though he was nothing but a dottering old fool.

After the Nazis left, he grabbed Lupo's wrist, just like he'd grabbed Volpe Rossa's in the park. "Don't worry about me," he said. "It's the young people. I told you before. They're the ones. Save them."

All the rest of the day, the old man's words played in Lupo's head.

That night Lupo lay in bed and stared at a spider on the wall, outlined in the moonlight. Save them—save the Jews—that's what this war was about. Sometimes it was hard to remember that. Sometimes it all felt pointless, a huge, sick game of running and hiding and killing and dying—for what?

Save the Jews.

Footsteps came running up the stairs.

Lupo jumped out of bed. But before he could hide, Volpe Rossa raced into the room, smack into his arms, trembling. He held her tight. His lips pressed into her hair. Something awful must have happened. He knew it would. He always knew it would.

Volpe Rossa had hated working indoors. It was too tame for her. She'd taken to delivering messages again. But she had no bicycle anymore. So she went by train, sometimes walking long distances on the other end. Today, though, the trains hadn't run.

When the trains didn't run, Volpe Rossa used another method. She'd go to the market and buy their biggest apple, cut it, and stuff the message inside. Then she'd stand by the roadside nibbling the apple. She got a ride from a German to her "uncle's," who was dying, or to her "cousin's," who just had a baby.

Lupo wanted to scream when the trains didn't run. He was always sure something awful would happen. And now it had.

He lifted his head away from her with difficulty and smoothed her hair. He was afraid to ask—to know. He hated facing the fact that he couldn't protect her. But maybe she needed to let it out. He sat on the bed, pulling her down with him. "Tell me."

Volpe Rossa turned around, so that she was still sitting in his lap, with her back toward his chest. She leaned her head beside his, and held her hands up in the moonlight in front of their faces. They glowed.

"We stole paint from a Nazi truck. You know, that phosphorous stuff they use to make the curbs at street crossings shine at night. We wrote on walls. We wrote 'Go home, Nazis.' We wrote 'Italy will be free.' We wrote 'Hitler is a criminal.'"

Lupo watched those glowing hands. Brave hands. Reckless hands.

They'd both become reckless.

"A patrol came along. Just one soldier." Volpe Rossa's voice grew fragile. Her hands stopped moving. "Three of us got away. But he caught one."

"They'll torture her." Lupo wrapped his arms around Volpe Rossa's waist.

"I wish I'd been the one to get caught. It's worse to know your friend is being tortured than to be tortured yourself."

"If you'd been caught, you'd have died. But she'll give up your names; she'll live."

Volpe Rossa put her hands over Lupo's. She didn't speak.

Her back was warm on his chest. Her cheek was soft against his.

He ran his chin along the part between her braids. Her hair smelled fruity, like woods after rain. "There's no time to lose."

"Ahhh!" shrieked Volpe Rossa, skittering to her feet.

Lupo stood in confused shame. "I'm sorry."

She pointed. "A spider."

A spider? Lupo shook his head disbelievingly in the dark. Then he laughed.

Volpe Rossa slapped his arm. "Don't laugh. I hate spiders. They have so many legs, and they crawl."

Lupo laughed harder. When Volpe Rossa went to slap him again, he grabbed her hand. "Put on your jacket. Do you need to bring anything?"

"What have I got?"

They crept down the stairs without a word to Alessandro's wife, their present host. It was better that she be able to show honest surprise at Volpe Rossa's absence when the police came.

· 23 ·

THE NIGHT STREETS WERE DESERTED. Lupo and Volpe Rossa hugged the walls, staying in the deepest dark, going from one narrow street to the next. Then they were outside town and immediately into fields. The ground was sloggy with late autumn.

"This way," said Volpe Rossa.

Lupo's chin jerked up defiantly. Volpe Rossa used to be the one who knew everything. But in Florence they'd become equals—she'd depended on him as much as he'd depended on her. Now, though, she took the lead again. It annoyed him. "How do you always know?"

"I don't in the daytime. But night is easy. The stars. It's not just a line in that *partigiani* song. It's true. *Partigiani* navigate by the stars and learn to judge long distances just with their eyes. Let me give you a lesson."

Volpe Rossa pointed out the constellations as they walked.

Then they sang. All Lupo's annoyance evaporated. They were a team, regardless of who was leading at the moment.

"We're far enough now," said Lupo. "We can stop to sleep."

"No. We'll travel by night and sleep by day. It's safer."

They continued up into the hills, climbing slowly, all night long. The land grew drier the higher they went. The leaves underfoot crunched now.

In the morning they came across a dirt road. It ended in front of a large home. Lupo headed for it. But Volpe Rossa caught him by the arm. "It's not a farmhouse. It's a country home for rich people. A second home."

"So what?"

"If there's anyone there, they're rich."

"No one's rich in Italy anymore."

"Perhaps you're right." Volpe Rossa dropped her hand. "But every *partigiano* I know comes from a farm or a factory, or used to work as a cleric in an office. We don't have houses like that."

Lupo rubbed his eyes. He felt like he could fall asleep standing. "Maybe there's no one there. Who goes to a country home these days?"

"Look at the chimney."

A faint curl of smoke rose there. Lupo felt stupid. "We could peek in the window—see who's there."

"We're not hungry enough or tired enough to take that kind of risk yet."

"Not tired enough?" said Lupo. "I can't get more tired than this."

"Poor baby boy," Volpe Rossa said mockingly. She gave a quick laugh. "You'll see. This is nothing. We've been pampered, living in cities for so long." She led him into the trees, to a pine grove littered with brown needles.

"Bed," said Volpe Rossa.

Lupo curled into sleep.

He woke to sunshine filtered through pine needles. It was a balmy day for early November. The storms of the past couple of months seemed to have ended. The air was placid. Then he realized what had woken him: a car motor.

Lupo crawled to the edge of the wood and watched a plume of dust thrown up by a retreating car.

He woke Volpe Rossa. "A car just left the house."

She yawned and rubbed her teeth with the side of her index finger. "Did you see how many people were in it?"

"No."

"There could still be people at the house. How hungry are you?"

"I'm thirsty more than anything."

"That cursed spider." Volpe Rossa stretched and got to

her feet. "If it hadn't been for that spider, I'd have thought to bring canteens."

Lupo found himself grinning.

"Stop that." Volpe Rossa flicked Lupo's arm with her fingers. "You could have thought of canteens. Anyway, I'm thirsty, too. We can't wait till night. Let's find a stream." She pointed. "Over there."

Lupo looked. He couldn't hear water, but the trees were thicker where she pointed. He followed her eagerly, his eyes taking in her slender back, the easy rhythm of her shoulders. He was so intent, he almost knocked into her when she stopped.

A middle-aged woman and a servant girl stood facing them. The woman held a bucket of water; the girl held two. The woman blanched. Then she put a hand to the base of her throat, in a gesture of relief. "You frightened me at first. Are you thirsty?" She held her bucket forward.

The servant girl fell back a step and silently mouthed the word no.

Volpe Rossa shook her head. Lupo did, too.

"Don't be shy. You must be. And I bet you're hungry, too. Come with us to the house."

Volpe Rossa gave an embarrassed smile. "My boyfriend and I had a little picnic in the woods." She picked twigs from her hair self-consciously. "We thought there might be a stream up here to dip our feet in."

"Don't be silly," said the woman. "It's too chilly for that. Come inside and have something hot to drink, at least." She stepped forward. Her skirt swung. The right side bulged at her hip. Was there something heavy in her pocket?

The servant girl mouthed, "No, no, no."

The woman's hand moved toward her pocket.

"Run!" shouted Lupo as he lunged. He caught the woman around the waist, and they fell together, overturning the bucket. Water sloshed across his back. A gun went off. He heard a scream. He flailed and found the woman's right arm. The pistol in her hand shone wet in the sun.

He rolled with the woman, disoriented at her unexpected strength. That scream had scrambled his brain. Who made it?

The woman bit him in the neck. She kicked. But Lupo finally wrested the gun from her and got to his feet, pointing it down at her. "Stay there." He stepped back, so she couldn't twist around and bite his ankle. He looked quickly behind him.

Volpe Rossa sat with both hands holding her side. She rocked back and forth in pain. He started for her. "No! Don't worry about me," she said. "Keep your eyes on her. Keep that gun on her."

The servant girl stood behind her mistress. She still held two water buckets. Her face was stricken.

"Listen," he said to her. "Help us or I'll kill your mistress. Do you understand?"

The girl nodded.

"When is the car coming back?"

"Not till tonight."

"Go get rope. Hurry."

The girl put down the buckets and ran.

"My husband's in the house," said the woman. "He'll kill you. Your only chance is to run for it now."

"Don't talk," barked Lupo. If there was anyone at the house, he'd have come out at that gunshot. They'd be dead already. "Lie flat."

"There's a rifle in the house. My girl will shoot you from the window. Run for it now."

Lupo was almost sure that girl wouldn't shoot them. She'd warned them, after all. But he couldn't give her away to her mistress. He pointed the gun at the woman's heart. "My finger's on the trigger. If a bullet hits me, killing you will be my last act. So you better hope she's smart enough not to shoot."

Volpe Rossa hummed in pain behind him.

"How bad is it?" he asked.

"Maybe not so bad. I think maybe it's just a graze. Not so bad."

The servant girl was quick. She brought rope and twine and tape and a bread knife.

"Help me or I'll shoot you both," said Lupo, for the sake of the show.

They tied the woman's ankles together, then her knees, then her wrists behind her back. They cut a rope for around her waist and another for around her neck and then tied the two together tightly, so that the woman's torso curved forward, and she couldn't look anywhere but down at her own body. They put tape over her mouth, and left her there.

Then Lupo lifted Volpe Rossa gingerly and carried her to the house. He set her down on the sofa.

The servant girl put the two buckets of water on the floor beside them. She ran and got soap and clean cloths.

Lupo cupped his hands and filled them with water. He held them in front of Volpe Rossa's mouth so she could drink. He filled them over and over.

Then he gently pulled Volpe Rossa's hands away from her side. He peeled up her bloody blouse. The bullet had hit in the side near her waist, and gone on by, taking a small chunk of flesh. It was more than a graze, but not much more. He'd seen a lot worse in the clinics. He washed the wound and doused it with the strongest alcoholic drink they had in the house—grappa.

Volpe Rossa screamed.

He pressed a clean cloth into the wound and taped it in place. "We'll need to take a little pile of clean cloths with us," he said to the servant girl, who had been watching him closely. "And the tape, too. And she needs clean clothes."

"You both do," said the girl. "Use the rest of the water in

this bucket for washing up yourself and your girlfriend, and I'll get you clean clothes. Then I'll make you a meal."

His girlfriend.

Lupo flushed. "You help her wash up and change. I'll make the meal."

The girl laughed in embarrassed surprise. "You cook?"

"Badly. But we're hungry, so it doesn't matter." Lupo carried one of the buckets into the kitchen.

From the window he could see the woman lying up on the hill, like a trussed boar. She rolled over as he watched. It clearly took a huge amount of energy.

Over to one side was a well. He didn't see anything else of interest.

He drank right from the bucket. He hadn't been this thirsty since that time he'd sat with Maurizio in Turkey, watching the house of the man who owned the yacht.

He set a pot of water to boil on the stove. The shelves held jars of tomatoes. He poured some in a pan and set it to boil, too.

"Here, let me take over." The servant girl came in. "Go wash yourself." She peeled two cloves of garlic and chopped them. "I couldn't find you any clean clothes, though. I'm sorry. The only shirts my master has in the house are black. I didn't think you'd want a Fascist shirt."

Lupo hesitated in the doorway. "You have a well. Why were you getting water from the stream?"

"The *partigiani* threw a dead cow down the well. By the time we got someone to pull it out, the whole place stank. My mistress thinks it's too polluted to use yet."

Lupo went into the living room. Volpe Rossa was leaning back on the sofa in a fresh skirt and blouse. In those fine clothes, she looked like a lady. She was gorgeous. "You look good."

"Wash your face and go find us some toothbrushes."

"How do you feel?"

"Hungry."

They ate a meal of spaghetti with tomato sauce, then cold, thinly sliced roast pork, then fresh pears. They packed a dinner of the rest of the pork, boiled potatoes, and a bunch of pears and nuts. And they packed a sack of cloths for bandages, and the bottle of grappa, just in case. And one bottle of water.

"Come with us," said Volpe Rossa to the servant girl.

"I don't want to. I've seen how the *partigiani* live. I can't do that."

"Wait till about a half hour before you expect your master home, then cut your mistress free," said Lupo. "Don't do it any sooner than that. We'll be moving slowly. Give us as much time as you can."

"Okay."

"She'll know we left earlier," said Volpe Rossa. She picked up a kitchen pan. "She has to believe you were out cold and you cut her free as soon as you could. Come here."

The girl put her hand over her mouth, but she nodded.

Volpe Rossa smacked her on the side of the head with the pan.

Lupo gasped as the girl reeled backward and fell.

She looked up at them with tears streaming down her face. The spot where she'd been whacked was deep red.

·24·

THEY WALKED SLOWLY the rest of the day. The stream ran north, so they stayed as close to it as the vegetation allowed. Lupo carried the food and bandages over one shoulder, shifting regularly. In his pocket the woman's gun lumped and thumped. Volpe Rossa didn't complain. She didn't make even the smallest whimper. They sang, and her voice was as strong as his.

They stopped at dusk to eat.

"You were right," said Lupo as he made a bed of pine needles for them to sit on. "The people in that house were Fascists. I've been thinking about it all day. Not all rich people in Italy are like them, though."

"Of course not. But richness isn't just a matter of money. It's how you think. The upper classes believe in order. That's what the Fascists offer." Volpe Rossa sat slowly, and then carefully lowered herself to lie on her good side. "Me, I like the creative exuberance of disorder." She laughed, then stopped with a wince. "Chaos, even."

Maybe there was no one in the world with more exuberance than Volpe Rossa. Lupo spread out the food.

"Do you think," asked Volpe Rossa in a small voice, "do you think there's enough grappa that I could drink a little? Just to ease the pain."

"Sure."

"That looks like a good meal," said a man, coming out from behind a tree. He spoke Italian with a German accent that made Lupo's neck hair stand on end even more than the rifle he pointed at him.

"Don't be alarmed," said another man, behind him, also pointing a rifle, this one at Volpe Rossa. He was Italian, and his accent told Lupo he was definitely from somewhere near Venice.

The combination of hearing a voice that gave him the sense of being in mortal danger and another that felt so familiar and friendly made Lupo dizzy.

"We've got these guns on you," said the Italian, "just to make sure you don't do something stupid like shoot us before you figure out what's up."

They were filthy. And skinny. But they looked strong, and their rifles didn't waver. Lupo put his hand on the outside of his pocket, but there was no point in going for that gun. These men would certainly shoot—and Lupo wouldn't.

"Put your gun on the ground," said the German man. "The one in your pocket."

Lupo couldn't believe he'd given himself away so easily. He lay the gun on the ground.

The Italian picked it up and put it in his own pocket. Then he sat down with his rifle across his lap. "Let's eat."

The German sat, too. "What is it?" he said to Volpe Rossa in a friendly way. "What happened to your side? Want to show me? I'm not bad at medical things."

Lupo bristled. "How do you know about her side?"

"We've been following you. She favors one side. She's obviously in pain." The German smiled. "You sing good. '*Wo man singt, da setze dich ruhig nieder, denn böse Leute haben keine Lieder.*'"

"'Wherever people sing, there set yourself peacefully down, for evil people have no songs,'" Lupo translated, for Volpe Rossa's sake. "Who are you?"

"Shall we do formal introductions?" said the Italian. He held out his hand. "I'm Struzzo—'Ostrich.'"

"And I'm Turbine—'Whirlwind,'" said the German.

Typical *partigiano* war names.

Lupo shook hands with each, hesitantly. "I'm Lupo."

Volpe Rossa shook hands with them, too. "Volpe Rossa." Did she trust them? Her face was unreadable.

The Italian picked up the small bundle of pork and politely held it out to Volpe Rossa. The German offered Lupo a potato. Everything had turned all crazy.

Lupo burst out, "What's a German doing with the resistance?"

The German stayed a moment, with his hand extended toward Lupo. Then he took a bite of the potato himself. "What's anyone doing with the resistance? I was in the army. At Dachau. Do you know about Dachau? Do you know what they do to the Jews there?"

"Is it a death camp?"

"A death camp." The German breathed tiredly. He took another bite of potato. "My people—my friends—my own brother, we worked in a death camp. Imagine it. I thought I was losing my mind."

Volpe Rossa raised her head with a jerk. "That's what Gufo wrote." She slowly worked herself up to sitting. "Those were exactly his words." She looked at the German with her lips parted slightly. Her face was sad wonder.

"Was he German?"

"No. But he saw things. Here in Italy. We both did."

"So . . . ," said the German. He finished the potato. "Thousands of us Germans deserted. Thousands of us are working for the resistance in these hills, and in the countryside of France, and in Germany and Poland. We aren't enough, but we do what we can to end this war."

And that's what Volpe Rossa herself had said to Lupo once. Maybe not the exact words. He couldn't remember spoken words exactly, like he could written words read over and over. But he knew she'd talked about doing whatever she could to end the war. This German sounded genuine, Lupo had to admit it, though he still felt off balance. There was something about this man that he didn't like.

"We're in need of new partners," said the Italian.

"Then I guess we came along at the right time," said Volpe Rossa.

The German laughed. "What a motley crew. One Italian man, one woman, one German, and a boy. Who's going to trust us?"

A boy? Lupo winced.

"They'll learn to trust us," said Volpe Rossa.

"Soffia il vento," sang the Italian.

"Urla la bufera," joined in the other three.

They sang as they ate, as they packed up, as they walked off into the night.

25

THEY BUILT A FIRE in the pattern of a gigantic X. It glowed bright in the frigid January air, a signal to an Allied plane, showing it where to drop supplies for the *partigiani*. Their assignment tonight was supply pickup. They'd built signal fires like this many times before. Supplies were dropped off on this hillside twice a month—so they felt secure in their experience; they knew how to do this job. They waited beside the fire: Struzzo, Turbine, Volpe Rossa, and Lupo.

The four of them had become an inseparable team. They went on so many different missions. They delivered arms to hiding places in gardens, helped prisoners escape from local holding points, dynamited strategic roads, sabotaged telegraph lines, delivered medicines and doctors' advice to makeshift clinics, brought food to women left alone with small children, passed messages with information about enemy troops and plans—anything and everything.

Other teams did all that and sniped at German trucks, too. But the band of *partigiani* they reported to wouldn't give Volpe Rossa direct battle assignments because she was a girl. That meant that the entire team of four never went to battle. Lupo was grateful. He wanted Volpe Rossa as far from battles as possible. And he wanted to reach home alive. And he wanted to do it without killing anyone.

So this work suited him well. He stood as close to the fire as he dared, for the warmth it let off, while still staying in the shadows. That was a rule: stay in the shadows unless you were forced out. He watched the sky.

The familiar drone came first. Then the plane was finally in sight. Supply boxes floated down on parachutes.

He was about to hurry toward where a box had landed when . . . Bang! Bang bang bang! From the dark all around Germans came running out, shouting and shooting. An ambush!

Lupo ran. He fell and got up and ran. He ran blindly, smacking into branches, tripping over rocks. He ran as hard as he'd ever run. Into the hills. Away.

He ran till he had no breath left. He stood, leaning forward, his hands supported on his thighs just above the knees. He couldn't hear anything behind him. No more rifle sounds in the distance. Nothing.

He went over what he'd seen in the split second after the first bang. Somebody falling. But he wasn't sure who. Not

Volpe Rossa, though. Someone taller. It could have even been a German, going down under friendly fire. Or maybe Turbine or Struzzo had taken someone down. They both carried rifles. Plus Struzzo still had the gun he'd taken off Lupo the first time they'd met.

He couldn't know now. He couldn't know anything till morning.

He sat with his back against a tree and finally fell asleep.

At dawn Lupo headed for the farmhouse. The team always had a prearranged rendezvous point in case of disaster, regardless of the kind of mission they were on. Anything could turn dangerous in a flash.

Like last night's supply drop.

But they were a good team, a lucky team. The others would be at the farmhouse waiting. Lupo knew they would.

A very good team. They were always hungry—who wasn't? They gnawed on bread that had turned black with mold. They slept on floors or muddy ground. They never had enough warm clothing. But Volpe Rossa's gunshot wound had healed well. And they had gone through the winter this far without the coughs and congestion that plagued the other *partigiani*. No matter how long they'd had to stay outside, even in sleet, they were always healthy.

The others would be at the farmhouse. They would.

And two were already there when Lupo arrived.

But Struzzo didn't show up.

They went back to look for him, walking separately, but always within hearing distance of one another. Turbine was the one to find Struzzo's body, hanging naked from a tree, tied up by one foot. Turbine and Lupo took turns digging the grave while Volpe Rossa patrolled the area in case the Germans came back. The frozen dirt made the job take hours. The shovel that the farm woman had insisted they bring with them clanked on rocks now and then.

At one point Turbine mumbled, "I wonder how many times she's sent a *partigiano* off with a shovel."

But Lupo didn't talk. He couldn't. He had grown close to Struzzo. Not really because of anything they had in common. Mainly it was just that he loved hearing him talk, hearing an accent that felt like home.

They lay the body straight in the grave, and the three of them stood on the edges in respect and sorrow. Struzzo's skin had turned gray with exposure to the bitter cold. Lupo had seen that before—in Ukraine, when both boys and soldiers died in the frozen winter. He'd seen it happen to his best friend, Samuele.

"I'm sorry," Lupo said quietly. "I'm sorry I don't have extra clothes to put on you."

"He wouldn't have accepted them," said Turbine. "If we had extra clothes, he'd want us to give them to other *partigiani*. To the ones who are still wearing summer shorts in the sleet."

A stab of hatred went through Lupo's gut. It made no sense to feel this way, and he knew it. Turbine was right. Turbine had turned out always to be right. Lupo should be grateful for that fact. It helped to have someone smart around.

Almost immediately they found another *partigiano* to band together with: Saetta—"Thunderbolt," so that they were a team of four again. But they changed their habits. From then on, only one of them built the signal fires and stayed at the drop-off point. The other three waited at a distance, then came up slowly to gather the supplies. That way if it was an ambush, they could try to ambush the ambushers. And Turbine and Saetta traded in their single-shot rifles for automatics.

Lupo had rebelled instantly to Saetta's name—for it felt as though the names themselves set Saetta and Turbine, the two that had to do with storms, against Lupo and Volpe Rossa, the two that were animal names. But Saetta quickly won him over.

Saetta was sixteen, only a year older than Lupo. They joked together. About nothing. They made each other laugh out loud. And they confessed moments of ignorance and fear. Saetta seemed to like Lupo instinctively. And he distrusted Turbine deeply. He never chose to sit beside the German at meals or lie beside him at night. He never entered into casual conversation with him.

Turbine noticed it. He offered Saetta food first. He did him little kindnesses.

But Saetta stayed firm against him. That alone would have been enough to make Lupo warm to the boy. But the friendship between Lupo and Saetta went beyond that. For the first time since he'd left Rina's farmhouse, Lupo had someone he could work beside without feeling any tension whatsoever. What a comfort that was—to care about someone with such ease.

They fell together in a natural rhythm, Lupo and Saetta walking or eating or working side by side, while the other two talked over strategy for their next mission. The more Volpe Rossa and Turbine paired off, the more Saetta and Lupo paired off.

One night when Volpe Rossa was up in the farmhouse helping their most recent farm family host and the guys were alone in the barn, Turbine said, "So, Saetta, tell me what they did to you?"

"What do you mean?"

"Something made you hate me. And it's nothing I did—we've had no quarrel. I'm used to working to earn the trust of *partigiani*. But I can't seem to earn yours, no matter what I do. What did my fellow countrymen do to you?"

Lupo blinked back his curiosity. It was more important to protect an honored tradition among *partigiani*, the tradition of privacy. "You don't have to answer, Saetta."

"That's right," said Turbine. "Our pasts are our own business. But your past could get in the way between you and me. We all depend on one another. And you and I are the only ones with rifles."

"Lupo's old enough to carry a rifle," said Saetta.

Lupo's stomach twisted. So far he hadn't had to defend his lack of a weapon.

"We're talking about you and me," said Turbine, to Lupo's relief. "About the problem between us. Maybe it will help to put it in the open." He folded his hands and locked eyes with Saetta. "If we don't have friendship, how can we keep up our spirits? And our spirits are our strongest weapons."

Turbine's voice was so clear, even Lupo felt compelled. He moved closer to Saetta to lend support.

"I stole a watermelon two summers ago." Saetta sat with his back against the barn wall. Now he rested his head against the wall, too, and looked up. "From a truck. The truckload was for the Nazi headquarters. An SS officer caught me. He drove me home, with the watermelon on my lap." Saetta spoke to the rafters. Though Lupo could see only the outline of his face in the dark, he sensed that Saetta was crying. "When we got home, the officer made me sit at the table until all my family got there. My father, my mother, my sister, my brother. Then he told them to sit, too, around the table. The SS officer made my mother cut the watermelon. The sweet smell filled the room. It was glossy red inside.

Perfect. He held a submachine gun. He told me to eat the watermelon. I ate. My little sister cried for a piece. We'd been hungry for so long. But the officer said it was my melon; I had stolen it, after all. I ate and ate while my sister cried. I puked. Then I ate some more. When I finished, he shot them. He killed my family. But not me. And he said, 'Let that be a lesson, dirty thief.'" Saetta stretched out on the straw.

Turbine and Lupo lay down, too. Lupo knew they were all crying.

Saetta's behavior toward Turbine didn't change after that. But Turbine no longer seem moved to try to change it. He let Saetta keep his distance.

And somehow Lupo knew that Turbine was right to let it go. Saetta couldn't make himself befriend Turbine, but he'd told Turbine his story. And that meant he accepted Turbine.

They were a team. They could count on each other. All of them.

·26·

MARCH BEGAN JUST AS COLD as the winter months before. Lupo shivered and hugged himself in the dark. He finished setting the fires for an Allied plane supply drop-off, then rushed back into the shadows beside scrub bushes and waited. This was a new drop-off point; Lupo felt skittish.

Turbine and Saetta and Volpe Rossa watched from a nearby hill. Whenever Lupo was the one to set the fires, he always had to squelch the urge to look in their general direction. He had to be careful not to give them away, in case anyone was watching him and saw where he looked.

He kept his eyes on the sky.

The familiar drone came. Then he saw the plane. But as it passed overhead, he made out only one parachute.

Clunk! So many clunks!

Lupo nestled back deeper into the bushes. What was going on? Was someone throwing things? Were there Germans in the trees over there?

He noted carefully where the single parachute had landed. That was important, otherwise it would be really hard to find it. He waited a good half an hour before he got up the nerve to go for it. Then he sneaked from bush to bush toward his goal.

He stumbled over something hard. He felt around in the faint moonlight. The pieces of a wooden crate lay scattered, with belts of ammunition between them.

Oh, he got it now: the other parachutes had failed to open.

By the time Saetta and Turbine and Volpe Rossa arrived, Lupo had made a pile. There was the box from the parachute that had worked, plus whatever contents he could gather from the shattered one he'd stumbled over. But he hadn't found anything else. He tried to remember how many clunks he'd heard. At least five.

The four of them searched the rest of the night for the missing boxes. Dawn came and they knew they should go back to their present quarters—another farmhouse. Daylight had become more dangerous than night in the hills, because the Germans now scouted for *partigiani* by day. And carrying supplies always took several trips; the supplies from just these two boxes would take a couple of trips. They should start right away.

But they couldn't stand the idea of German scouts finding those other supplies.

They kept searching.

When the sun was overhead, Turbine ran across Lupo. "Let's get the others and carry back what we have."

Lupo agreed. He was dead tired. And clouds had formed to the east. The wind was picking up. It might rain. They should get those supplies back to the farmhouse fast.

Turbine whistled. That was their secret call. It was supposed to sound birdlike.

In a few minutes Volpe Rossa showed up.

They waited.

Turbine whistled again.

Saetta didn't come.

They spread out looking for him. But finding a person in these hills was as hard as finding a box that fell from a plane. They didn't dare call out his name.

They met up in half an hour, as they'd planned. Volpe Rossa had come across another smashed box of supplies, but most of the rifles in it had been destroyed on impact. They followed her to it and brought back whatever they could salvage. Then Volpe Rossa and Turbine loaded their arms with what supplies they could carry and headed back to the farmhouse. Lupo kept searching for Saetta.

He climbed to the closest high peak and stared in one

direction for about ten minutes, hoping to spot movement. Then he shifted his gaze by a few degrees and stared in a new direction. It took him more than an hour to scan a full circle.

This wasn't possible. People didn't just disappear.

Lupo whistled. He was lousy at it. It didn't carry far, not like Turbine's whistle. The rain had started, and his lips were so cold. Chills shook his whole body. But he tried again, with more force. He whistled and whistled. He knew it was stupid to keep it up. Anyone who heard would know that wasn't a bird. Any Nazi hiding in the trees.

There could be Nazis hiding anywhere. Everywhere.

Was that a German helmet, or just a treetop? Was that a German signal, or a real crow caw? Every rustle sent him spinning this direction and that.

Now he saw movement in bush branches. He hurried toward it, as silently as he could. But it was just Volpe Rossa and Turbine, returning to pick up more supplies.

"Come with us," said Volpe Rossa.

Lupo shook his head.

Volpe Rossa put her hand to Lupo's cheek. Her head tilted to the side; her eyes held all the sadness in the world.

For an instant the only thing Lupo wanted was for her hand to stay there, on his cheek, forever. Nothing else mattered.

But her hand fell.

Turbine and Volpe Rossa left.

Lupo walked in straight lines now, or as straight as the cover of bushes allowed. He went back and forth, sweeping the area, like he'd seen German planes do. He came across a fourth box of supplies—this one with nothing at all salvageable.

And no Saetta.

He kept searching, watching over his shoulder, jumping at every noise, but searching anyway. Nothing could make him give up.

When Saetta had failed to appear at Turbine's first whistle, a sense of dread had danced at the very edge of Lupo's consciousness. By now that sense of dread had grown monstrous; it slammed its way through his thoughts. He looked up into the trees. He looked for a body.

He stomped on in the rain, searching through branches, stumbling over rocks. Looking, looking, looking. The rain pounded.

The next thing he knew, Volpe Rossa was pulling his arm across the back of her shoulders. Turbine did the same to his other arm. They helped him to his feet.

He must have fallen asleep. He pushed them away. "I'm okay. I have to find Saetta."

Volpe Rossa took his hand. "They probably got him."

"What if they didn't? What if he's hurt and waiting for us to find him?"

"If he's hurt only a little, he'll find us. Or other *partigiani*. If he's hurt bad, he'd want us to leave him. Just like I'd want you to leave me. This is our job, Lupo. We have to get back to work." She pulled him tripping after her. They returned to the farmhouse.

They never saw Saetta again.

At first they didn't want any more new partners. It felt unlucky to have a fourth. Volpe Rossa was adamant; she said they shouldn't doom anyone else.

But it was too hard to do everything with only three of them. Four allowed them to split into partners for all sorts of tasks. So they soon banded together with Pecora—"Sheep." He was short and stocky, but he was fast on his feet and a hard worker. And he barely spoke.

When they did pair off, Volpe Rossa insisted on taking Pecora as her partner—as though she thought she could better protect him. She made Lupo think of those little dogs that yap at bigger dogs, thinking they're so tough.

Or maybe it was something else—something even more heartbreaking. Maybe she was protecting all the men—this way, if something terrible happened to Pecora, neither Turbine nor Lupo could blame himself. Lupo had to look away when Volpe Rossa would choose Pecora as a partner for fear that she'd see the guess in his eyes. The tough one—Volpe Rossa was always the tough one, all-business. She'd hate being revealed.

One night in April it was Pecora's turn to build a signal fire. This was an extra important mission because they expected an extra large supply drop. The American President Roosevelt had died the week before. But instead of that causing a pause in the Allied war effort, the new President Truman was sending the *partigiani* more and better supplies than ever: ammunition, automatic rifles, machine guns, 45-millimeter mortars. The Brits were giving more, too.

Lupo stood on a nearby hill with Turbine and Volpe Rossa and scanned the area below for the flaming X.

"There! See it?" Turbine pointed.

The three of them fastened their eyes on that spot, trying to memorize recognizable trees and rock outcroppings from where they were to that X. They were supposed to wait till the plane passed. Then they'd slowly make their way to the signal point, going from landmark to landmark.

They had to go slowly in case Germans had seen the signal and were swarming the area. They were determined that no German would ever get the chance to ambush them again.

They were looking in concentrated silence at the signal fire that Pecora had set, when, oh no, they saw a second flaming X, a few kilometers to the west.

Lupo knew instantly what had happened: a German decoy. Just a few days ago the Germans had set a decoy for another Allied plane supply drop-off. Spies had infiltrated the *partigiani* bands in these hills. Everyone had suspected it. But now it was definite.

There were still men who had served in Mussolini's army at the start and remained loyal to the Fascists. Not many. Someone said it might be ten thousand at most. But that was enough to cause problems. The Nazis never could have spied successfully on the *partigiani* without the help of Italian Fascists.

Someone Lupo had known, someone he had maybe talked to, maybe shared bread with, had betrayed them. And now here they were, on the brink of who knew what.

But what was to follow couldn't be too awful, it couldn't be. It was a luscious spring night. The air was sweet with honeysuckle. The breeze refreshed. Night birds tapped out mating calls. Bats swooped, then rose again, with leathery beats of their wings. It was way too fertile a night to be the stage of a disaster.

Lupo moved closer to Volpe Rossa to reassure her. This would end well; he had to believe that.

"All right," said Turbine. "Here's what we do."

He was taking charge. Again. No one had put Turbine in charge of them; he'd developed the habit on his own. And Volpe Rossa didn't seem to mind. Usually Lupo did, though. But not tonight. Tonight he wanted someone else to be responsible. He wanted Pecora's fate to lie in someone else's hands. He listened closely.

"We run toward whichever X the plane flies over. If it's the decoy, the Germans will be waiting. You both hang back while I go in shooting. As soon as I've killed a few, there will be guns for you, too. We'll fight them for those supplies. And if it's the real X, our X, then we can be sure the Germans will be rushing over soon. But at least you two can pick up guns from the new batch of supplies. Either way, tonight's a battle."

Lupo's first battle.

They stood in a line, watching.

"We might as well sing," said Volpe Rossa. "A whisper song, at least."

They sang "Bella Ciao"—"Beautiful Good-bye"—that song about *partigiani* dying for liberty. Don't let it be prophetic, Lupo prayed silently. Let it be a charm against itself.

The hum of the airplane came before they finished the first stanza. Parachutes floated down toward the enemy decoy X. They ran flat out.

· 27 ·

"WHY AREN'T YOU A MEMBER of the Fascist Party?" The Italian prison guard stood with his back to the door and an automatic rifle hanging across his chest.

Volpe Rossa stood facing him. She put her hands on her hips. "You asked me this yesterday, when they threw me in here. Three times. And again this morning."

"And I'll keep asking till you answer, foolish girl. If you'd had a member card on you, we could have found a place for you to sleep separate from these scummy men. Maybe you wouldn't even have been locked up at all. You're stupid not to be a member."

"I will tell you a story," said Volpe Rossa. "Have you ever heard of Angelina Merlin?"

"No."

Lupo hadn't heard of her, either, but her name sounded Venetian. He'd been half dozing on the floor in the corner. Now he perked up.

"She was arrested in 1924 for anti-Fascist activity and stayed in prison five years. Then she was arrested again almost twenty years later. They asked her why she wasn't a Fascist Party member. She said, 'Do you know the date of the origin of fascism? I do: March 23, 1919. Today is May 19, 1943. If I am not a member, it is because I am not a Fascist.'" Volpe Rossa sat on the end of her cot. "It's almost two years later, but my answer is the same as hers."

"That kind of talk is dangerous," said the guard. "You'll get labeled rebels, rather than the bandits that you are."

"Bandits? We're not bandits."

"If you ask me, you're crazy," said the guard. "Be glad we're shorthanded enough that they postponed the real interrogation for a day. Otherwise you'd be writhing in pain now." He pulled on the tip of his mustache and looked down at Volpe Rossa like an angry father. "If you play your cards right and listen to what I say—if you let them think you're bandits and stop saying stupid things—then you'll get out eventually. Rebels, ha, they get shot. And they deserve it. They should all be shot, like Hitler wants; none of them is smart enough to save his skin by giving information. They don't even wage war in a sensible way. No banners. No valor. You don't want to be associated with them."

"How can you possibly know who I want to be associated with?"

"Look at you. You're a pretty girl. And you're young.

You've got your whole life ahead of you. What are you doing running around all filthy, with lice crawling on you, dragging around that boy—who's big enough to be shot, by the way—and, worse, the mute?" The guard pointed at Turbine, asleep on his cot. "He looks to be an idiot, too. He sleeps through everything. How on earth you entrusted a rifle to an idiot, no one will understand. You better figure that one out before they interrogate you. It was stupid. They would have shot him right there in the woods when he wouldn't give his name if you hadn't shouted he was a mute. They told me." He made a tsk and threw up his hands in disgust. "Bunch of overgrown headstrong children—that's what the rebels are. The oldest of them are hardly in their twenties. See them." He jerked his chin toward the other people in the prison cell—four *partigiani* stretched out on their cots, staring at the ceiling. "If you change your mind and want to act civil to me, I might be able to keep you from the interrogations. I could even get you out sooner. Your father must be so ashamed."

"Look who's here," said Volpe Rossa.

The door had opened behind the guard. A girl of about ten years old stood there. Lupo didn't know her name. She hadn't said it in front of him. She came yesterday at the same time—noon—right after those four other *partigiani* came back from their torture session. And she carried the same large basket in her arms.

"What have you got in there?" asked the guard.

"Clothes for mending. I gathered them from neighbors, and I have to bring them to my grandmother," said the girl. "After I visit my uncle."

This was a lie. The basket was filled with food and water. And the guard knew that very well. But he pretended to be ignorant. The other prisoners had explained: it lowered tensions between the prison workers and the townsfolk to know the *partigiani* weren't starving, at least. Things were about to explode around here; everyone had joined the resistance.

Yesterday the basket had held a water bottle filled with brandy, as well. The four *partigiani* had drunk till they couldn't feel the pain from their torturing.

The guard left. That was part of the routine, too. He wouldn't come back till he was sure they had finished eating. At least an hour.

All seven prisoners—Volpe Rossa, Turbine, Lupo, and the four other *partigiani*—came forward and sat in a circle around the girl.

"You're going to make someone a fine wife someday," said one of them.

"Me," said another. "Marry me."

Lupo had heard it all before. These prisoners had been hooked to an electric shock machine just this morning. They were doomed. Yet they kept up the banter with the little girl. They laughed at their own jokes till she smiled.

And there was Lupo, barely able to keep from crying, when no one had laid a hand on him. They got caught before Turbine could even fire a single shot. Caught and tied up and marched off to this prison.

Lupo had no idea where Pecora was. Turbine said he was dead. Either that, or he'd been the one to betray them. A Fascist. Whichever, he was dead to them.

"Did you help cook today?" the third prisoner asked the girl lightly.

"I love your cooking," said the last one. "And especially how sweetly you fill a water bottle."

The four of them laughed.

The girl shook her head. "Strip," she said. "Hurry." She opened the basket and passed out trousers and shirts. Nice clothes. The kind of clothes an ordinary person would wear, not a *partigiano* who'd been living in the hills for months on end. There were seven outfits.

"And here." The girl took out a shaving razor, a hairbrush, scissors, and a mirror.

Volpe Rossa grabbed Turbine by the elbow, and they jumped into action. She cut one of the *partigiano*'s hair while Turbine shaved him, and the rest of them looked at the sizes of the clothes and figured out who should wear what. They dressed and used their own spit to try to clean their faces. Then Volpe Rossa and Turbine processed the next *partigiano*, and the next. They were a synchronized pair, brushing past one another easily, snaking their arms through one another's intimately as they worked. They cleaned up all the prisoners, including Lupo. Finally, Volpe Rossa cut Turbine's hair while Lupo stepped in to shave him.

Then Volpe Rossa put the scissors in Turbine's hands, and, without missing a beat, he cut her hair. Those wondrously thick curls—gone. How had Turbine known so fast that that's what she wanted him to do? With trousers on, she looked like a thirteen-year-old boy. It shocked Lupo what a good disguise it was.

Volpe Rossa scooped up her cut locks and tucked them away inside her shirt in one sweep of her hands. Lupo understood; no telltale locks could be left behind. If they actually managed to get out of here, the police would be looking for a girl, not the boy she now appeared to be. She was so smart—all the time thinking.

Everything happened quickly and silently. The seven of them moved like a single animal. The beast of the resistance. It felt right to Lupo, natural, inevitable.

They put on hats, tilting them this way and that to cover electrocution burns. They put hands in pockets to hide missing nails.

"Act like you're the king," said the girl, with her hand on the doorknob. "That's what my mother said. No one stops a king." She opened the door.

They walked out. Turbine took the girl's free hand. Her

other held the basket. They didn't even know which way to turn, but the girl did; she guided them.

Lupo put his hands in his pockets so he'd look just like the others. This couldn't possibly work. He'd heard about all kinds of prison breaks, but nothing as obvious as this could work. Two of them shuffled, they'd been hurt so badly this morning. And all of them had hollow eyes. No one could think they were anything but prisoners. They'd get shot. And that girl, that little child, she'd get shot, too.

She led them down a corridor, across a lobby, out past the entrance guard. Lupo's mouth and throat were so dry with fear, they scratched. He almost gagged, holding in a cough. But the guard hardly gave them a glance. It was visitors who entered that got inspected, not visitors who left.

The prison was a converted school in the middle of the town of Modena. Lupo linked his arm with one of the slower *partigiani*, and Volpe Rossa linked her arm with the other. The group walked more quickly now and turned down the first street. Two *partigiani* bolted.

"Wait," called the girl. "This way." She ducked into a house.

But those two had already disappeared down an alley. The remaining five pushed through the door behind the child.

Girls around Volpe Rossa's age huddled in the living room.

"Who wants to be my beau?" said one of them, stepping

forward. "I know a nice walk we can take. And a good place to end up at, with people who can help you get back out in the hills. We must walk slowly. We're out of work and we're lovers, after all."

"Slow is just my speed." A *partigiano* offered his arm.

She looked at him as she might look at a lover. And he somehow seemed handsome, transformed by her look.

They went out the door.

Another girl stepped forward. "Who wants to work at the bakery with me this afternoon? It's not that hard, and you get hot bread. Afterward, I'll take you to the same end point."

The other *partigiano* smiled. "They don't call me Mangiapane—'Bread Eater'—for nothing." He followed her out the door.

Only Lupo, Volpe Rossa, and Turbine remained.

"You," said a girl, stepping up to Lupo, "you'd make me a fine little brother. We can walk to my house, quarreling, if you want."

"I'm not leaving her." Lupo moved to Volpe Rossa's side.

"People walking alone, with a clear purpose—they do okay. Pairs manage, too. But once you've got three together, the police stop you if the Nazis don't."

"Then you take her as your little brother," said Lupo, jerking his chin toward Volpe Rossa. "She looks the part better than me, anyway. I'll follow alone."

The girl frowned.

"Wait," said the little girl who had led them out of prison. She left the room and came back with a pair of soccer shoes and an old soccer ball. "Can you fit in these?"

Lupo put on the soccer shoes.

She handed him the ball.

"Stay far enough behind that no one connects you to us," said the older girl, who already stood by the door with Volpe Rossa in tow. "If you lose us, go to the main piazza and wait. Someone will come by for you later."

"I don't know where the main piazza is."

"You'll find it. The Nazi headquarters are there, in the big hotel. Just follow an SS officer."

"What about him?" asked Volpe Rossa. She pointed at Turbine and locked eyes with him.

"I have a hiding spot big enough for one till nighttime," said the little girl. "Don't worry."

The older girl pinched Volpe Rossa in the arm. They left, arguing loudly about who was supposed to do an errand for their grandmother. They sounded just like a sister and brother.

A few minutes later, Lupo went out the door and followed them, kicking the ball against the walls and around parked motor scooters. He dribbled it from foot to foot. It had been years since he'd played soccer, but it felt like yesterday. He used to play in the Campo Santa Maria Formosa in Venice with his big brother Sergio. Half the boys from his part of Venice played there almost every day.

The girl and Volpe Rossa turned, out of sight. Lupo's heart flipped. He fought the urge to run after them. He dribbled fast to the corner. There they were, turning another corner.

A policeman turned the same corner but coming toward Lupo. He pointed his finger and headed right at him.

Lupo did the only thing he could think of; he passed the ball to the policeman.

The policeman jumped in surprise, but he automatically kicked it back. They passed that ball up and down the empty street for a good half an hour. Then another policeman came running up and talked to the first policeman. The first policeman told Lupo to get off the streets, because prisoners had escaped and they'd be questioning everyone.

"Yes, sir." Lupo picked up the ball and ran down the street Volpe Rossa and the girl had taken. They were nowhere in sight, of course. He couldn't keep running; that would attract attention. He put down the ball and dribbled.

Before, back when they were in the prison, Volpe Rossa and Turbine and Lupo had agreed that if they ever got free, they'd meet up in the barn of the first farmhouse to the north of town, taking the main road. The other four *partigiani* had told them the family there would help them. That's probably where the two *partigiani* who had bolted were headed right now.

But the girl who had gone off with Volpe Rossa had said to go to the main piazza, and someone would come for him later. He'd be with Volpe Rossa sooner that way.

The question was, where was this famous piazza?

German soldiers came running down the street toward Lupo. He bounced the ball against a wall with his head. Bonk, bonk, bonk. He could still do it—after all this time. Bonk, bonk, bonk. The Germans ran past, talking fast. But it wasn't about a prison break. Lupo made out something about fighting in Bologna. Open battles. The uprising must have been spectacular from the level of the soldiers' excitement.

He ran into the first coffee bar. The bartender looked at him with quick alarm, then seemed to relax again. People huddled around a radio. Lupo stood by a wall and listened. The Allies had been fighting in the Po River Valley for ten days. A day ago, April 19, open fighting had broken out in Bologna. It was the *partigiani* against the Nazis and Fascists. But the Allies were coming. They would be there by the next day at the latest.

Lupo crossed his arms over his chest. Did he dare believe it? The Allies had been supposed to come for so long now.

But everyone else seemed convinced. They talked happily, all at once. Florence had been liberated way last August while poor Bologna, fewer than a hundred kilometers to the north of Florence, was still occupied. All that would be over now. They congratulated one another.

Let it be true. Oh, Lord, let it be true. Those good people that Lupo knew and had worked with in Bologna, let them be free. If Allies and *partigiani* fought side by side, they'd win. They couldn't help but win. The radio said the *partigiani* had killed over one thousand Nazis in Bologna that first day of fighting alone. Imagine what they could do if the Allies were with them.

Just five more days and it would be Lupo's sixteenth birthday. Maybe he'd actually celebrate it with his parents. Lord, let it be.

"It's our time, too," said a man. "Modena's hour. If we make it so. It's up to us."

The cry to arms went from person to person, and the coffee bar was suddenly empty, but for Lupo. Even the bartender had disappeared, going into a back room.

A moment later he returned with two rifles. He handed one to Lupo. Then he went behind the bar counter, reached underneath, and set two large canvas sacks on the counter. He opened one; it held cartridges. He loaded his rifle, filled his pockets with cartridges, and went out the door into the street.

This was it. They were going to fight for Modena. For

freedom. For dignity. There were no more messages to carry or supply boxes to pick up or telegraph lines to tear down. The job was with that rifle.

Lupo loaded it. He put cartridges in his pocket. Then, on second thought, he put an entire sack over his arm. He moved as though he knew what he was doing, but he felt like he was dreaming.

He went out into the street and ran, staying close to the building walls. He heard shots ahead and came out on a piazza. A German truck was parked beside him. He shot out the tires. It was an act without thought—but, oh, it was the perfect way he could help. He felt awake again. He ran up and down the streets, shooting out the tires of German vehicles.

A bullet whizzed past his head.

"Here!" A girl of maybe twelve opened a door and pulled him inside. She locked the door. "Go upstairs and shoot from the window. Shoot from my room."

Lupo took the stairs two at a time, his heart banging like a wild thing in a box. He knelt by the window of the girl's room and shot at tires as jeeps and cars and trucks went past. After each shot, he flattened himself on the floor till the barrage of retaliatory bullets ended. Then he got back up and shot at the next vehicle's tires. Shots came from other windows, too. Shots came from everywhere.

Lupo finally hit a tire.

Now a jeep clogged up the traffic. No other vehicles could come down that narrow road.

If he was going to be useful, he had to find a way to shoot at vehicles on other streets—so he could clog them, too. He had to get himself in a position to see those streets without having to pass by the jeep he'd debilitated out in front of this house. And, oh, he knew exactly how to do that. He was from Venice, after all, and all Venetian boys knew how to get around the city without ever touching the ground.

Lupo ran downstairs and found the girl in the kitchen, cutting bread.

She handed him a slice, and a chunk of cheese. "I was going to bring it to you. You didn't have to come find me."

"How do you get out onto the roof?" Lupo asked, stuffing his mouth with the heavenly food.

The girl ran ahead of him up the stairs, up a second set, and opened a door.

"Thanks so much."

"Wait," she said. "Kiss me first."

He stared a moment, stunned. He kissed her, one tentative kiss. Then he ran along the roof to the next home, and the next. He ran over the connected roofs till he got to the end house. From here, he could see the road that ran perpendicular to the one blocked by the disabled jeep. It was a bigger road, and a German truck rumbled along it. But he was a poor shot. He'd never hit anything at such a distance.

Still, he knelt, aimed, fired. The front right tire of the truck blew. Just like that.

He lay flat on the roof.

Bullets zinged past. He heard screaming and shooting. A loud crash. A grenade.

He ran back along the roofs to the other end. It overlooked the next street perpendicular to the one blocked by the jeep. He shot. He shot and shot, till he finally blew out a tire.

The street on one side was narrow, but nowhere near as narrow as the alleys of Venice. It would be impossible to jump across to the next block. So he ran along the roofs, scouting the streets below. Finally, the jeep he'd crippled before was rolling again, with a new tire. He shot out another tire.

He passed the day that way, shooting out tires every time he heard traffic start again on one of the three streets he could aim at. In between, he lay on the roof and stared at the sky. The city exploded around him in intermittent battles. His upper-right chest hurt from the recoil of the gun. His neck ached from bending over the gun sight.

Eventually the sack of cartridges ran out. And eventually night came. The sound of bullets stopped. It was time to find Volpe Rossa.

He returned to the house of the girl who had helped him

before. The girl who'd given him his first kiss. The roof door was unlocked. He went down the stairs as quietly as he could, rifle in hand, and out into the street.

There were no streetlamps on. And the moonlight didn't make it to the ground, the buildings were so tall and this street was so narrow. He hunched over and ran in the dark, turning onto whatever street seemed bigger. A patrol of German soldiers marched back and forth in front of a building on a piazza. This must be the Nazi headquarters. Lights were on inside.

Lupo hid in the shadows and scanned the piazza. He moved slowly along one wall, to get a better view of the whole place.

"What took you so long?" A boy came up beside him. It was Volpe Rossa—still in disguise.

Turbine was behind her. "With those soccer shoes, we expected you to be faster."

"Come on." Volpe Rossa scurried down one street after another. If a noise came from the left, she went right. If a noise came from the right, she went left. No matter what, she kept moving. Eventually, they emerged on the edge of town.

They ran into a field and didn't stop till the houses were far behind.

"Here's our choice," said Turbine. "We can stay and fight.

There's no doubt that the Allies will finish the job in Bologna by tomorrow at the latest. Then they'll head this way. The skirmishes of today were nothing compared to what's going to happen. Modena will be free within two days, mark my words. We can be part of it."

Volpe Rossa touched the rifle in Lupo's hands. "Do you think you can use that?"

"I've been using it. I've blown out tires. Give me another cartridge and I'll blow out more."

She smiled. "Good work."

"What are you two talking about?" asked Turbine. "You mean Lupo won't kill anyone?" He put his hand on Lupo's shoulder. "Listen to me, Lupo. The one who survives is the one who shoots first. I can't take you into battle if you won't use that rifle."

Lupo brushed Turbine's hand off his shoulder. "I take myself wherever I go. I use this rifle however I choose."

Turbine hung his head and shook it. He looked off into the night. Then he looked back at Lupo. "You're right."

"You said we have a choice." Volpe Rossa crossed her arms at her chest. "What's the other possibility?"

"We can head toward the Veneto, where the Nazis are still strong," said Turbine. "And we can help where they need it even more."

"I know Lupo's vote," said Volpe Rossa. "I vote with him."

"Then we're unanimous." Turbine picked up the rifle he

had set on the ground when they stopped. "You have a birthday soon, right, Lupo?"

"April 25."

Turbine took a cartridge out of his pocket and handed it to Lupo. "An early present. We better hurry if we're going to see Venice liberated in time for your cake."

· 28 ·

BY LUPO'S BIRTHDAY, all the things Turbine predicted would happen did. And more. Bologna was liberated on April 21, Modena on April 22, Reggio and Parma on April 24.

Meanwhile, on the northwest coast of Italy, the *partigiani* came down from the hills and took over Genoa. British planes had dropped arms to them, but much got destroyed in the drops, and what was left was little in comparison to what the Germans had. The *partigiani* mounted broken machine guns on roofs just for show. And still, by grit and determination, they prevailed. By the time the Allies arrived at the city on April 26, Genoa was already liberated—by the ragtag resistance.

Lupo learned about these things from the occasional radio and, mostly, by word of mouth among *partigiani*. That was their lifeline—any bit of promising news. Everyone was at the breaking point, but news like this kept them whole.

As Lupo turned sixteen, the north of Italy was almost entirely liberated. Some said April 25 should become the Festival of the Resistance, a day to be celebrated every year, as marking the victory of the *partigiani* and the end of occupation.

But not every place was free yet. Not the place that meant the most to Lupo.

The three of them—Turbine, Volpe Rossa, and Lupo—had come to Padua and were working with the *partigiani* right in the city. They got here partly walking, partly hitching rides in cars on back roads. For days they worked on fortifying strategic locations. By night they put up posters on walls of public buildings telling the Nazis and Fascists to surrender; the end was at hand.

The Nazis got in trucks and made for the Alps. But the *partigiani* had seized the bridges over the Brenta River, cutting off that escape route.

On April 27 the trapped Germans decided to ruin Padua. It was like a repeat of what Colonel Scholl's troops did to Naples back in September 1943. They blasted the city with heavy artillery fire, even though they knew they'd have to give it up.

But this time the people fought back immediately, and in overwhelming numbers, before the city could be reduced to rubble. They captured German soldiers and locked them in a huge barrack. The Germans wound up shelling that barrack and unwittingly killed hundreds of their own men. By the end of the battle, over 20,000 German prisoners were taken.

Through all this Lupo shot tires. He crippled dozens of German trucks, cars, jeeps, scooters.

The night of April 27 many *partigiani* headed north, chasing after the escaping enemy in the provinces of Treviso and Belluno. But Lupo, Volpe Rossa, and Turbine walked the main road toward Venice, wretched Venice, still occupied.

They walked in the center of the road, because the retreating Germans had scattered mines through the grasses. It was the Nazi mantra Lupo was way too familiar with by now: do as much damage as you can, even in defeat, or, maybe, especially in defeat.

Lupo recognized nothing on either side of the road, of course. Still, the terrain felt familiar. He didn't know if it could possibly be true, but he thought he smelled the sea. The lagoon. The place he'd swum as a boy—what seemed ages ago.

Mamma would be asleep now. She'd have the window open, because she liked a chill at night. It made her sleep better. Papà would be curled in a blanket beside her, because he hated to sleep cold. And his brother Sergio? Was Sergio still off somewhere in Germany?

Lupo breathed hard. He was exhausted from the day. His eyes burned. His feet stung. His shoulders ached. But a new kind of energy surged through him. He was almost home. At last.

"I've never been to Venice," said Turbine.

"Neither have I," said Volpe Rossa. "Tell us the layout, Lupo."

"I don't know where to begin. It's nothing like any of the cities we've worked in together. There are canals everywhere."

Turbine laughed. "Well, everyone knows that."

"Halt!" A German soldier jumped out from the ditch on the side of the road. He pointed a submachine gun at them.

Another ran from the ditch across the road, holding a pistol in front of him.

"Don't shoot," shouted Turbine in German.

"What? You're German? I just heard you speaking Italian. All three of you."

"I'm a spy," said Turbine. "And they're Fascists."

A truck came up a side road. It stopped. "Get in," called the driver in German. "Shoot them and get in."

"The man's German. He says he's a spy. He says the two boys are Fascists."

"Shoot them and get in."

"But he's German."

"I'm Austrian, and even if he was Austrian, I'd shoot him."

"I won't shoot a German spy."

"Do whatever you want. Just get in! We have to go fast."

The soldier with the pistol collected their rifles. The one

with the machine gun made them climb into the back of the truck. Then the two German soldiers climbed into the back behind them.

The truck crossed the main road and went up back roads, heading north.

It was too noisy to talk in the open truck bed. And the sides were too high to see anything. The truck kept going and going. It was slow, this beat-up truck, but it was steady. With every minute it put more distance between Lupo and his home.

And he'd been so close!

This couldn't happen. He couldn't let it. Not now. He stood up.

The German aimed the submachine gun at him.

Turbine yanked him back down.

Volpe Rossa closed her arms around his chest from behind. She held him tight.

The truck rumbled along as dawn came. Now the road wound up into the foothills of the Alps. They were heading to Austria. No.

The motor coughed. And died.

It started again, coughed, died.

"Damn!" The driver came around to the back of the truck, holding a semiautomatic rifle. "We're out of gas."

"Then they'll capture us," said the soldier with the pistol.

"I know this area. I know a place we can hide, past Asiago.

If Italians come in little groups, we can kill them easily from there. We can kill plenty before we're captured. Come on."

They tramped through the woods. The driver led the way. One soldier kept his pistol in Lupo's back. The other kept his machine gun aimed at Turbine's and Volpe Rossa's backs. Flowers sweetened the air with all the zest of spring. Lupo swallowed his sour saliva.

After about half an hour the driver said, "Here." He stopped at a hole and pointed down with his rifle. "We killed plenty at this spot last winter. Then this spring the Italians killed plenty of us. They even threw in Italian whores who slept with our officers." He turned his eyes on Volpe Rossa and Lupo. "So now it's our turn again."

The other two soldiers edged over and peeked into the hole. They coughed and put their hands over their nose and mouth. "What a stench!" the one with the submachine gun said.

Lupo knew this place. He'd never been here, but he'd heard about it. Venetians called it the Buso. But its name in Italian was Buco della Luna—"Moon Hole." It was a natural rock formation, a type of cave, he guessed, with its opening at the very top.

"How far does it go down?" the one with the submachine gun asked.

"I'll show you." The driver looked at Turbine. "You really German?"

"Yes," said Turbine.

"So you're a spy?"

"Yes."

"Prove it. Push the short guy in." He pointed at Volpe Rossa, who was still dressed like a young boy.

"No!" Lupo stepped forward.

The soldier with the pistol jammed it in his face. "Stay put."

"They're Fascists," said Turbine. "Both of them."

"They're Italian," said the soldier with the submachine gun. He pointed it at Volpe Rossa.

A spasm zipped through Lupo so hard, his nose brushed the pistol barrel in his face. He had to protect Volpe Rossa. No matter what.

"Push the short guy in," said the driver. "Then we can force the other guy to jump. They might be Fascists, but I'm sure they're dirty Catholics. So if the short guy doesn't die right off, the other guy will kill him when he falls on him." He smiled with satisfaction. "He can commit murder and suicide at the same time. A double sin for a Catholic."

Turbine grabbed Volpe Rossa by the arm.

Lupo opened his mouth to shout when—what?—Turbine kissed her. Turbine kissed Volpe Rossa. And she kissed him back. They loved each other. And Lupo hadn't even known. Or maybe he had. That's why he'd been so annoyed with Turbine all along; he'd sensed it. From the very first encounter, something had sparked between them. Oh, yes, he'd known. Volpe Rossa kissed Turbine. His Volpe Rossa.

The soldiers were as astonished as Lupo. Even more so, because Volpe Rossa was dressed as a boy. They stood there, jaws dropped.

Lupo sprang. He snatched the pistol in front of his face and shot the soldier holding the submachine gun. That soldier slumped forward over the gun.

Someone jumped on Lupo's back. It was the other German soldier, the one Lupo had grabbed the pistol from. They rolled in the dirt. A rifle went off somewhere. A machine gun hammered the air. Lupo didn't know who was shooting, who was being shot. Nothing made sense. He was rolling with this soldier, rolling and kicking and fighting and—

"Aaaaaah!" screamed the soldier as he slipped into the Buso.

A tremendous jerk came on Lupo's shoulder.

The soldier dangled in the Buso, holding on to Lupo for dear life.

Lupo felt himself being dragged into the hole by the great struggling weight on his arm.

Bang!

The soldier went limp, let go, fell.

29

TURBINE AND LUPO CARRIED Volpe Rossa's body back to the road. The ground was too rocky here to dig a grave without the right tools. Their tears had stopped. But they still didn't speak.

The bodies of the three Nazis were at the bottom of the Buso. When Lupo had looked down it in the morning sun, he had seen other bodies there. Lots of them. Italian bodies and German bodies, stinking as they rotted.

The two of them walked in tandem along the road. Lupo was in front, holding Volpe Rossa by the knees. Turbine held her by the armpits.

Her body was stiff with rigor mortis. It didn't carry like a body, but more like a strangely cut piece of wood. Lupo felt a sense of unreality as they walked. How could this thing, this object, be Volpe Rossa, the one he loved?

They went south. The pistol in Lupo's pocket lumped and thumped. That's what guns did. He hated it. But it still held one bullet. He had used the other one. And that sense of unreality came again. How could Lupo be the person who had killed a man?

The other German guns were back at the Buso. Turbine had emptied the submachine gun into the driver, the one who had shot Volpe Rossa. Then he'd picked up the driver's rifle and shot the Nazi Lupo was struggling with. It turned out to be the last rifle bullet.

A single bullet could change so much.

Why should Lupo be surprised? That's how it always was—how life always went. Single things changed everything. A single person, a single kiss.

They stopped at the first country house. The woman inside fed them soup and bread. She gave them two shovels and led them out back, showing them where to bury Volpe Rossa. Beside two other fresh graves.

They dug without pause, deeper and deeper. It wasn't like they'd talked about putting her so deep no wild animal from the nearby forest would ever be able to dig her up. It wasn't anything rational or planned. They just kept digging.

Turbine finally put down his shovel and jumped into the hole. Lupo lowered Volpe Rossa into his arms. Turbine lay her down and smoothed her clothes, her hair. He worked to straighten her legs, to fold her arms on her chest. But her body was so stiff and hard, it was impossible. Turbine didn't stop, though. He pushed and pulled and pushed and pulled, till

Lupo jumped down into the hole and wrapped his arms around Turbine from behind so he couldn't move—like Volpe Rossa had wrapped her arms around Lupo in the back of the German truck. And they cried. They just cried. They just cried.

And everything was real again.

Oh, Lord.

When they left, they walked side by side.

Night came. They slept in the grasses. In the morning they came to a town. They learned that just the day before, Mussolini had been shot in a piazza in Milan. They learned that on that same day the people of Venice had rebelled. They'd captured ten thousand prisoners and lost only three hundred of their own men. Venice was free.

They hitched a ride south, down through little towns that were cleaning up, washing away blood, burying the dead.

When they reached the main highway, Turbine went west. Volpe Rossa's sister lived that way—in Bergamo. She had told him. She had told Turbine about her family, when she'd never told Lupo things like that.

Turbine would go there now and let Volpe Rossa's sister know what had happened. Maybe he'd stay there. Maybe he'd make it his home.

Lupo hugged him good-bye. No, not Lupo. He was Roberto again. The war was over. The beast of the resistance would disperse. He could try to find himself again, if any of him remained. Roberto.

Roberto hitched a ride on a truck full of Americans. They took his pistol away. That was fine with him. He never wanted to hold a gun again, ever.

They told him the Eighth Army had been assigned to liberate Venice that day, but since Venice was already free, they were going in to help restore order.

Order. What could the word mean? Roberto's life had been without order for so long.

The truck rode along the highway that crossed the lagoon. Ibises picked their way with dainty feet. The names of all the seabirds came back to Roberto. The names he'd learned from Randy, the American soldier back in North Africa. Birds came and went, year after year, migrating with hope of better weather, better life. They believed in order. They kept going.

That's what life was—keeping going.

Roberto had been in other trucks like this. So many trucks, boats, trains, wagons in the past three years. He'd bicycled and walked and run such a long distance.

He stood up in the back of the truck. No one yanked him down this time. He looked ahead. That was his city over there. People he loved were waiting for him. He gripped the side of the truck as it rumbled along.

POSTSCRIPT

AT THE END OF THE FIRST WEEK OF MAY 1945, the German government unconditionally surrendered, and the war in Europe ended.

Of the 7,013 Jews who had been deported from Italy to death camps, only 830 of them lived to come back. Of those Jews who remained in Italy, 303 more died of mistreatment or suicide.

Over 200,000 *partigiani* were formally enlisted in the resistance army, and many more people who were not formally enlisted fought—like the Roberto/Lupo, Teresa/Volpe Rossa, and Turbine of this story. Additionally, there were countless ordinary citizens who did their part without ever picking up a weapon. At least 40,000 of those formally enlisted died, but there is no way to accurately count the full number of Italians who died in the resistance.

The particular events that happened to Roberto/Lupo in this story are fictional, though most are fictionalized accounts of events that happened to others during this period. I tried to stick to real happenings as often as possible to pay tribute to the staggering self-sacrifice and courage of the *partigiani*.

If you would like to hear tunes of the resistance songs and learn more about the resistance and activities that celebrate the memories of the *partigiani*, please visit the Web site of the Associazione Nazionale Partigiani d'Italia: http://www.anpi.it.

To hear the tune "Bella Ciao" and learn the words, go to the Web site: http://ingeb.org/songs/bellacia.html. This is undoubtedly the most well known of the resistance songs.

If you would like to learn more about and hear the tune of the resistance song "Fischia il Vento," please visit the Web site of the Parco Culturale "Il Sentiero di Fischia il Vento" in the region called Liguria: http://www.liguri.net/portAppennini/pak_fv.htm. To learn the words to the song "Fischia il Vento," go to the Web site: http://ingeb.org/songs/fischiav.html. You'll find that the version given there begins with the words *"Fischia il vento"* ("The wind whistles") instead of the *"Soffia il vento,"* given in this story. Popular songs have many different versions. In this story, I chose to give the version best known to my friends in Venice, since Roberto is from Venice.